# THE COMEBACK

Also by Annie Zaidi

*City of Incident: A Novel in Twelve Parts*
*Bread, Cement, Cactus: A Memoir of Belonging and Dislocation*
*Prelude to a Riot: A Novel*
*Gulab*
*Love Story #1 to 14*
*The Good Indian Girl*
*Known Turf: Bantering with Bandits and Other True Tales*
*Crush*
*3 Plays: Untitled 1; Jam; Name, Place, Animal, Thing*

Books edited by Annie Zaidi
*Unbound: 2,000 Years of Indian Women's Writing*

# THE COMEBACK
a NOVEL

Annie Zaidi

ALEPH

ALEPH

ALEPH BOOK COMPANY
An independent publishing firm
promoted by *Rupa Publications India*

First published in India in 2025
by Aleph Book Company
7/16 Ansari Road, Daryaganj
New Delhi 110 002

Copyright © Annie Zaidi 2025

The author has asserted her moral rights.

This is a work of fiction. Names, characters,
places and incidents are either the product of the
author's imagination or are used fictitiously and any
resemblance to any actual persons, living or dead,
events or locales is entirely coincidental.

All rights reserved.

No part of this publication may be reproduced,
transmitted, or stored in a retrieval system, in any
form or by any means, without permission in
writing from Aleph Book Company.

ISBN: 978-93-6523-672-9

1 3 5 7 9 10 8 6 4 2

For sale in the Indian subcontinent only.

Printed in India

This book is sold subject to the condition that it
shall not, by way of trade or otherwise, be lent,
resold, hired out, or otherwise circulated without
the publisher's prior consent in any form of binding
or cover other than that in which it is published.

*To the girls with whom I ganged up to found Spectrum, and to my beloved theatre colleagues*

There were five missed calls. By the time I got around to calling Asghar back, it was past midnight but he wouldn't mind, I was certain. We often talked into the wee hours even on weekdays. He never said a word about having to be up at six in the morning and dropping the kids off at school at a quarter to eight. My own brother might say something like, *some of us have real jobs, you know?* Not Asghar.

I used to get drunk a few times a year and call him, raving and ranting about how I was passed over yet again, the injustice of it, and how I was sick of everyone, mostly myself. Asghar would get me through the night and into the pale dawn of a new day. Me pouring myself cheap gins, him rooting about in the fridge for a midnight snack. He didn't get fat, no matter how many kebabs and cream rolls he ate, and his eyes never failed to crinkle when I called him a good-looking bastard with his head of curls, hazel eyes, and lanky frame. If he spent any time at all in the gym, he'd have the kind of torso that sells business suits. He could sing and I bet he could dance, too, if he took lessons. I, on the other hand, with my short legs, big nose, and square jaw, would never turn any heads. Yet, I had ended up the actor and Asghar, the bank manager.

It could so easily have been the other way around. Asghar had a better grip on literature and stagecraft. I had a better head for math. But then, I cleared high school with less than 80 per cent marks and all hopes of getting into engineering college died. Not that I especially minded. I didn't particularly want to be an engineer, or, for that matter, a banker. Because my own father was a banker, I had signed up for a Bachelor's in commerce but my first week on campus, I ran into Asghar and I never attended a lecture again. Asghar and his group of friends had founded an undergraduate theatre club in Baansa and I had started acting only because he picked me to play the lead in the club's first production. That's all I had been trying to say in the *Buzz* interview that set off a storm and blew all our boats off course.

For over fifteen years, I had hung about on the

fringes of Bollywood. While I waited for my big break, I did whatever jobs came to hand. Plays, theatre lighting, bit parts on television, radio jingles, audiobooks. Fifteen long years of auditioning for meaty roles but, zilch. Then a film producer happened to listen to a Hindi novel that I had narrated. He didn't just buy the adaptation rights, he insisted I play the narrator's role in the film. This character was supposed to be an unattractive guy, fortyish, and with a mean streak, and the producer thought that I looked and sounded the part. The film was shot on a low budget. I was paid peanuts but the day I was invited to see the rough cut, I knew, from now on, things were going to be different for me. And they were.

The week the film released in theatres, *Buzz* called about doing a profile. Now, a profile is already different from merely being interviewed. First, the magazine sent a photographer who shot my face with some love, bringing light to its creases, gouging the hollows under my eyes even deeper. There I sat, holding a book under a lamp, cast into shadows that made me look like a man of obscure and dangerous origins. There I was again, leaning against a balcony railing in a rumpled night suit. Unwashed, unbrushed, almost sexy.

**The Comeback**

Then a journalist came over to interview me. She insisted on visiting me at home because, she said, she was looking for *texture*. So I made her a cup of tea and talked about growing up in a small town called Baansa, north of Lucknow but south of Bareilly. How I'd cut classes to meet girls, how swirls of dust rose up in the first week of June and how they filled your nostrils and throat until you felt as if you'd choke to death, and how December brought a sort of rolling fog that blinded you and made you jump at the sound of footsteps so that you started to believe in ghosts. That sort of thing.

The journalist sat cross-legged on my carpet, her eyes twinkling. She said, 'Reeally?' so often that I began to warm up to the texture of my own life. I told her about a skinny river that bends at a forty-five-degree angle, and about the townsfolk who affectionately call it Burhiya: the old woman. I talked about bicycle rides through bamboo groves, and a fledgling drama club at a mofussil university. I told her about my best buddy, Asghar, and how he had prepared me for the stage, and how, in the final year of college, I had climbed up a drainpipe to stand on a window ledge and help Asghar during his Economics exam. Oh, that profile was going to sparkle with gravelly detail. They'll put all that stuff in my obituary some day, I thought.

The day the *Buzz* profile was published, my phone was ringing non-stop. I was on the cover of the magazine. Casting directors were calling to ask about my schedule and would I mind auditioning? Of course, they already knew I was perfect for the role, but would I mind reading some lines and filming myself on my cell phone? I got offered an advertisement for ginger cookies. Sejal, my ex-wife, sent champagne. There were calls from theatre friends, uncles, journalists wanting more anecdotes about my long years of 'struggle'. Asghar's five missed calls were part of that mix and I didn't answer because I wanted to talk to him at length and with no interruptions.

When at last I did call back, he didn't answer. Could he be asleep? Quite likely, I thought, for it was the middle of the week. I went to bed and woke up late the next morning and was promptly distracted by more calls from industry folk. At the end of the day, my brother Aun sent me a text, asking if I had spoken to Asghar. So, I tried calling again, before midnight this time.

Asghar answered after several rings but he didn't say a word. Not even hello. I kept saying, 'Hello?

Aggu? Are you there? Can you hear me?'

At last he spoke. 'I can hear.'

His voice was so quiet, I knew at once that something was wrong. Still, I strutted about for a couple of minutes, wanting to talk of my own triumph first.

'Your protégé finally made it, huh? How do you feel about that?'

It was an old joke of ours, me being his 'find'. His was the hand that had picked up a rock and polished it into a gemstone. Asghar always said that whenever I got my big break, I should make sure to tell everyone that he had been my first mentor and champion. But now that the day had arrived, he was silent.

'What's going on, bhai?' I asked. 'Were you sleeping?'

The silence stretched thin over the phone, then dissolved into a series of heaves and sniffles. It took me a while to figure out that the man was weeping.

Now what's a man to do when another man does that? I've done my share of messy calls but I never cried on another fellow. I stood barefoot in the kitchen, a glass of gin in my hand. I took a small sip and waited for an explanation. Could he be drunk? But, no, Asghar didn't drink and he never ranted. He had little to rant about anyway. Steady job, pretty wife, nice kids, mother in good health. Last we spoke, his wife Zubi had brought home a kitten. His older girl, Afsana, was a teenager and the younger one, Tarana, had just hit double digits.

'Are things at home okay? Is your mother okay?' I asked.

More silence, then some sniffling. I quaffed the whole drink in one gulp.

'Don't fucking freak me out, Aggu. Say something!'

Asghar hung up. I called back at once and this time, it was Zubi who answered. Turned out, my best friend had just gotten fired because of my *Buzz* interview. The last few months, Asghar had been having a rough time at the bank where he worked. One of his senior managers was intent on shunting him off to Agra in a market development role and Asghar had declined. He hated market development and, besides, he wanted to stay on in Lucknow. That's where Zubi's parents lived and that's where his girls went to school. The trouble was, everyone at his bank already knew that Asghar and I had studied together at the Aalha Udal Mahavidyalaya in Baansa. He had often mentioned me at work, and had even boasted about being best friends with the actor John K. Reading my interview in *Buzz*, his colleagues had immediately guessed that he was the same Asghar who had needed my help to pass his Economics exams. His manager promptly wrote a formal complaint, challenging the educational credentials on the basis of which Asghar had been hired. He was fired overnight.

With the taint of 'cheating' hanging over his undergraduate degree, Zubi said, it would be impossible for Asghar to get hired at any other bank. There was rent to pay, two kids in school, a kitten to feed. She demanded that I make things right. After all, it was my braggadocio that had landed them in this mess. She wanted me to announce in public that I had made up that story about cheating during our college exams, just to add some colour to our otherwise drab life in Baansa.

For a minute, I stood there blubbering. I said 'Shit' and 'I am so sorry!' over and over. I asked to speak to Asghar and he came to the phone reluctantly.

'Aggu,' I said. 'I didn't think... *Shit!* I'm such an idiot. You know I'm an idiot, right?'

He remained silent. I begged him to swear at me, to abuse me as much as he wanted. In the background, I could hear Zubi saying, 'Cut the crap. Ask him to say it was a lie.' And then, I found myself saying,

'But, yaar, it's too late to take it back, no? I mean, who'd believe me now?'

A long pause and then Asghar said, 'You're right. It is too late.'

**The Comeback**

I drank myself stupid that night. My long-delayed moment of triumph had been ruined. I tried to call Asghar again the next morning and when he didn't answer, I started texting him every few hours. He didn't even read the texts. Finally, I left a voice note, apologizing profusely and offering a loan to tide him over a year. I had just been signed onto a couple of new projects and he could take everything I had, for as long as he needed. He sent a text with the single word: 'No.'

'You have the kids to consider,' I texted back.

He wrote back: 'Everyone has someone to consider. If they want to consider other people at all.'

After that day, Asghar stopped responding to my texts and calls. It was as if he was building a wall of silence around himself and I thought it best to keep my head down for a few days. It was a busy time anyway. I devoted myself to signing more contracts and making the most of my moment. A week passed, and then Cheeku called to ask: did I know that Asghar was back?

Cheeku had been part of our college drama club even though he couldn't act, couldn't write, couldn't sing or dance. He was clumsy and short-sighted too, so he couldn't be trusted with lights or props in the dark. He was, however, in love with drama and he had a decent head for numbers, so he was given charge of budgets and ticket sales. All the other members of our drama club had left Baansa for higher studies or jobs. Cheeku was the only one who stayed because his father owned a prosperous sweet-and-snack shop that he had inherited as an only son. He didn't mind sitting at the shop. If accounting was what he was going to do with his life, why not do it at home?

The drama club was dead but Cheeku had tried to keep his link to the theatre alive by sponsoring an annual drama competition for college students. The Aalha Udal Mahavidyalaya offered its stage, a concrete platform under the open sky that was otherwise used only twice a year for flag-hoisting, patriotic songs, and ceremonial speeches. Cheeku's sponsorship involved free snacks and sweets to all contestants and five thousand rupees to the winning team. The rest of the year, he occupied himself by reliving memories, keeping in touch with all his college friends, and posting photos of Baansa on social media. He also made sure to watch any film or TV show I was in, even if I had just five seconds of screen time. Then he'd call to let me know how proud he felt. But I had never heard him sound as excited as he was the day he gave me the news that Asghar was back.

'What do you mean, back?' I asked.

'Back means *back*! Back in Baansa!'

Turned out, Asghar had been summoned home by his mother. All of us had always called her Shakeela ma'am. She had taught Mathematics at the state higher secondary school for thirty-two years and, when she retired from the job, her former students who now had kids of their own, began to insist that she continue to teach at home. Children in Baansa always needed extra coaching in English and Math. Because time hung heavy on her hands, and also because she didn't like the prospect of accepting money from Asghar in case she fell sick or felt short of her savings, she started to offer home tuitions. Behind her back, everyone called her the 'Sixty Percent ma'am'. She made no claims about helping kids score 90 per cent marks, but she did promise that any student of hers would score at least 60 per cent. Desperate parents sent their kids, the ones who were borderline failing, and asked her to save them. So did the ambitious parents of kids who were already scoring well, but who needed an extra nudge to crack the entrance to engineering degree colleges.

Shakeela ma'am did not read magazines like *Buzz* and she didn't hear about the fallout of my interview from her own family. Some of her pupils had shared the magazine article over WhatsApp and one of the more intractable kids had asked outright why she couldn't make her own son a 60 percenter.

At first, Shakeela ma'am didn't quite believe it. She told herself that film folk cooked up falsehood for a living, and Jaun had just let his imagination run amuck. She waited for her son to call and say that it was all a crock of lies, but Asghar had not called her for over a week. At last, she called her daughter-in-law to ask, what's all this she's hearing? And Zubi started to curse my selfish heart.

'What can I say, Amma? That cursed Jaun doesn't care... It's not like *his* job needs an economics degree.'

The older woman's hands were shaking when she put away her phone. And at this point, I thought Cheeku was giving himself some artistic license. After all, he was not present when this conversation took place. But he insisted that he had a reliable eyewitness account from Bittu, his chief fryer of samosas. Bittu, of course, was also not an eyewitness himself. He got the story from Mullan, who cooked and cleaned for Shakeela ma'am, and who took pride in recounting every whisper and gesture, every bit of gossip she picked up. In her own words, Mullan believed in using her sharp eyes, ears, and tongue because that's what God had given her, and what son-of-a-mortal dared suggest that she should not be using her blessings?

Shakeela ma'am, Mullan reported, had issued an order: Asghar was to come home at once. Then she sent Mullan off to Cheeku's shop for namakpara and milk cake. Asghar drove down from Lucknow with Zubi and the kids. She greeted them, fed them, allowed the girls to open her storeroom and rummage inside old trunks filled with fifty-year-old garments and smelling of naphthalene. Then she called Asghar into the room that she used for tuitions. She wanted to hear it from his own lips—was Jaun telling the truth? Had he cheated in his college exams?

Asghar snapped, 'Is *that* your chief concern, Amma? Whatever happened, it was nearly sixteen years ago!'

Shakeela ma'am always had a wooden cane handy. There was a time she had travelled in rickety state transport buses and the cane had helped to send out a signal: she was not afraid to use a cane on anyone who misbehaved, be it in the classroom or outside. Now, she picked up that cane and asked Asghar to stand up straight.

He spoke irritably, asking if she too was missing her job, and she dealt him a blow on the back of his legs. The first howl was involuntary. She asked him, again, to stand straight. This time, he obeyed.

Hearing the thwacking sounds from the next room, Zubi came running, followed by the children. But Shakeela ma'am was like a woman possessed. She delivered blow upon blow and although Asghar didn't utter a sound, his daughters were screaming, cowering, clinging to their mother. It was only when Zubi ran to hug Asghar and the blow landed on her daughter-in-law's body that Shakeela ma'am's cane fell from her hands. Red-faced, gasping for breath, she staggered to the wall and burst into tears.

Once she recovered use of her tongue, it was hard to make her stop. She declared that Asghar had left her no face to show in town. Over three decades of making an honest living, eating cold lunches out of a battered tiffin box, travelling by bus so she could teach children to solve problems through logic and reason, and telling parents she could make any child pass their exams with a respectable score. But look at her own son! Her son's cheating translated into her being a liar. Who'd believe that he hadn't cheated in all his exams right through? And why on earth had he picked economics if he had no head for it? Did she ever say that he couldn't study history or literature? Had she been a bad mother? Then why did he punish her with such disgrace?

Shakeela ma'am was one of a handful of mothers in town who had had to double up as a father, and Asghar was her only child. Yet, she never told him to become a doctor or an engineer, or a government official. Life had taught her that men, even the good-looking, sweet-tempered ones, keeled over suddenly and left their wives to deal with hospital bills that sucked the life out of them. Life was unpredictable and only Allah could know the future. The only thing she did ask was that Asghar never do anything to shame her. And look now! All her pride had been washed away, she said.

When Shakeela ma'am began to beat her own head with her hands, Asghar rushed towards her, grabbed her wrists and began to weep. Zubi stood weeping in another corner. Tarana and Afsana were already crying and since Mullan was the only one left, by her own report, she too started to cry.

Shakeela ma'am wept until she started to grow breathless. For a while, things looked dire. Water was fetched, her palms were massaged, and she was carried to her bed. Once she had fallen asleep, everyone crept into separate rooms to nurse their separate wounds.

For two days, nobody stepped out of the house. Shakeela ma'am lay curled up in bed, doubly ashamed now for having beaten her grown son in front of his wife and children. The girls huddled together, talking in whispers and timidly helping themselves to bunkebab when they got hungry. Asghar stayed in bed too, one arm thrown over his eyes so nobody could see the tears as they came rolling down. Zubi made endless cups of tea, leaving them quietly at his bedside. She washed the dishes herself and dusted every surface in the house, just for the sake of having something to do, and this upset Mullan for she thought of the kitchen as *her* domain. Finally, it was Mullan who barged into Asghar's room to complain.

'Bhaiyya, I may as well stop coming to work. Nobody eats anything. There's nothing to wash.

Dulhan seems not to like my work.'

Asghar sat up, rubbed his palms over his face, and he mumbled something about pink Kashmiri tea. Mullan wondered if his mind had been touched. Pink tea was only made on special occasions like weddings, and it was always made in a giant vat for dozens of guests. On the other hand, it was also made at funerals. Mullan couldn't guess at what was running through his head but, at least, she had a chore in hand and she welcomed it.

An hour later, Asghar carried in a tray filled with fragrant, steaming cups of pink Kashmiri tea into his mother's bedroom. Dulhan Zubi followed, carrying in plates stacked with namakpara, and the girls followed with a low table.

Shakeela ma'am lay with her face turned to the wall. Asghar began to massage her feet. Then he asked Afsana to pop bits of namakpara into his mouth, and asked Tarana to hold a cup of tea to his lips. He blew on the rim and drank it up with such loud slurps, the girls started to giggle. Then he began to tell them stories about how their grandmother made fierce eyes at him if she ever heard him making a noise while eating and drinking. He, of course, had not taught his daughters anything and as a result, they had horrible manners. He demonstrated some of those noises now, and the girls giggled some more.

'Still,' Asghar said, 'there's only one thing my Amma forgot to teach me. How to say "no". I could never say "no" to my friends. Couldn't say "no" to my own fear. I wanted to study the arts, but there wasn't a single artist in Baansa. The only painters here are those who paint shop signs and houses. I wanted to study literature, but the bookstores here never sold anything except school textbooks. I got interested in drama but the only theatre artists I ever met were part of a travelling group. They came from Bareilly once a year, for the Ramlila. I still remember that air of hunger and compromise they carried around. How cheap they sold their time and labour! They put in weeks of rehearsal, travelled hundreds of kilometres, and all for what? A few hundred rupees as honorarium and one large room where the whole group slept together. So, I decided, art wasn't for middle-class people like us. I would study economics or business management. I'd get a real job. Theatre would be a pastime, a shauq for weekends. And yet, from the moment I founded that drama club in college, the stage consumed me. The texts, the readings, the challenge of transforming a bare concrete platform into anything I wanted. I loved it. I loved every single thing about it. And then, there were my friends, Jaun especially. He was hungry to be on stage and his hunger stoked mine. He did cheat in every exam. Didn't attend a single lecture. But he had his whole life mapped out. He was going to be an actor and he would get his parents to pay for a proper drama school. All he needed was a little help from me. Just one more play, Jaun begged me. And I couldn't say "no" even though it was right before the final exams.'

All of this was true. Three months before our final-year exams, I was begging Asghar to direct a new play. The New School for Performing Arts in Mumbai offered an acting diploma that was rated among the best in the country. The only hitch was that you had to show evidence of having been part of seven amateur or student productions. Failing that, they wouldn't even look at your application. I had already acted in six of Asghar's plays. If I could do just one more show, I could be on my way to becoming a real actor, and straight on track to Bollywood movie stardom. If only I could get into the New School diploma programme, I thought, the rest of my life would be as smooth as a well-made tiramisu. And so, I pestered Asghar to put on another show.

At first, Asghar had baulked. He said he needed to study for the exams, especially Economics. But I had laughed away his worries and promised that he'd pass with distinction. Dozens of students helped each other during exams, passing notes, sending texts on hidden cell phones, standing on a window ledge near the windows to supply answers to tough questions. It wasn't a particularly original idea. Lots of students did it, in lots of towns and villages. In fact, it was the only sensible course of action, I argued. Anybody could write an Economics exam but only Asghar could direct a fine play. Besides, it was our last year in college. It would be the last time he'd get to produce and direct a show. Didn't he want to put up something memorable? Heck! I even offered to study in his stead. It was a travesty anyway, wasn't it? The individualism of the examination system crushed the collaborative spirit out of students.

I chipped away at his reluctance until Asghar caved. He spent that winter crafting a brilliant adaptation of *Mudrarakshas* in Urdu, and I played a fine contemporary Chanakya. And when it was time for his Economics paper, I got up there on the ledge and gave him answers to questions he needed help with. Quid pro quo, I had thought.

'Rotten fellow, your Jaun! He didn't say all that in the interview, did he?'

Shakeela ma'am was sitting up in bed now. She accepted a cup of pink tea and drank it as noisily as she could, to show her granddaughters that she wasn't above a joke.

'And why on earth,' she asked, 'does he spell his name as John K.?'

'He was afraid Jaun Kazim would be less appealing to the masses,' Zubi sniffed.

'Forget Jaun,' Asghar said. 'Jaun doesn't matter. What's important is that I fix this. Amma, I promise, you will hold up your head again. I'll pass my exams. Legit pass.'

As Shakeela ma'am reached out for her son's face and kissed him on both cheeks, Zubi bit her lips anxiously. She had steeled herself against the loss of Asghar's job, but a student-husband was a whole different matter. Her own instinct was to ask her father for a loan to tide the family over until her husband could find another job or set himself up in business.

'How will—' she began to say but Asghar stopped her. He folded his hands in a gesture of supplication and begged Zubi to hold the fort for a year. She could finally put her fancy MBA degree to some use, he said.

As long as she stayed in her mother-in-law's house, Zubi managed to wear a smile but she had very different ideas about fort-holding in a marriage. She had met Asghar while studying for an MBA degree and the two got married soon after. Asghar already had the bank job and she never felt the need to look at recruitment advertisements or attend job interviews. Then the children came. Starting a career at this late stage felt impossible to her, not to mention, impractical. As a thirty-six-year-old with zero work experience, how much money could she expect to make? She wasn't going to put herself out there for petty cash, she told Asghar.

It was finally agreed that Zubi should move into her parents' house in Lucknow so the children could stay on at school. Meanwhile, Asghar would stay on in Baansa and sit for his Economics exam again. They had, however, underestimated the complexity of the problem. Aalha Udal Mahavidyalaya would not allow him to re-sit just the final year papers. He would have to re-enrol and re-sit all his exams for all three years of a Bachelor's degree. He would have to start from scratch.

Shakeela ma'am said there was no shame in taking a step backwards. However, alert to Zubi's misery, she also added that there were millions of people out there who made a living without a college degree. But now Asghar was adamant. He would not resign himself to merely making a living. He would not sell insurance or work in a shop. He bit the bullet and enrolled at the National Open University to study English literature.

Over the phone, Zubi asked where he thought he'd go with a literature degree? He'd be nearly forty by the time he was done and he'd need a Master's degree too, if he wanted a decent teaching job. How long would *that* take? Five years?

Over the phone, Asghar asked if she had applied for any jobs herself. Both fell silent, and then Asghar asked if the children were doing alright, and then they hung up.

Both were jobless, so they didn't meet very often. Travelling between Baansa and Lucknow cost money, after all. Besides, Asghar couldn't imagine going to his in-laws' house empty-handed. He had always visited them very briefly, and each time he went, he was loaded with gifts. Now he couldn't bear to show them his jobless face. As for Zubi, she couldn't visit Baansa too often because…well, she just didn't.

When Cheeku called me next, I was in the middle of a shoot, trying not to appear lecherous while holding up a piece of candy and lip-synching to a jingle that went, 'Can't help myself, ta-na-na-nah.'

Cheeku's voice was so shrill with excitement, I had to hold the handset several inches from my ear. Asghar, he yelled, has started a new theatre company. And it's not college theatre. It's *theatre* theatre! Did I hear that? Theatre *company!*

I distinctly recall feeling a peculiar sensation in my lower back, a tightness in my calf muscles. I could hear Cheeku saying, 'Hello? Hello, are you listening?' and I found myself disconnecting the call. I would make up an excuse later, pretend the phone had run out of charge. In that moment, I couldn't quite trust the words that would come out of my mouth.

'Pretty cool,' I said later. 'Typical Aggu move. You

never quite know what to expect, huh? So damn cool!'

'He's the coolest, bro!' Cheeku crowed.

I bit down on a note of irritation. It's almost as if he had a crush on Asghar and I really wished he wouldn't say 'bro'. An unkind thought popped into my head: how cool could theatre possibly be, in a place like Baansa? But aloud, I only said, 'Keep me posted, Cheeks!'

Cheeku being Cheeku, and also because he had nothing to do at the shop except accounting and some quality control, which he did by tasting his own goods, dutifully kept me posted. The minute he heard that Asghar had registered Act II Drama Company as a business, he wanted in. He counted out the day's takings at the sweet shop, pinched his ears apologetically before a photograph of his late father, and handed charge of the till to Bittu. Then he ran off to meet Asghar and offered to finance the company's first play. But Asghar turned him down.

'Don't give me money, bhai,' he said. 'If you're serious about wanting in, help me make money.'

Asghar needed someone to handle marketing and ticketing and, if the company turned a profit in its first year, then Cheeku was welcome to come on board as an equal partner.

As Cheeku relayed the conversation to me, the word 'profit' made me laugh. Profit from theatre? In Baansa? For its maiden production, Shakeela ma'am had stepped in as producer. Food, costumes, and props were her responsibility. Her living room was the company office, and all parts of the house were rehearsal space. I was all too familiar with this mode of production. As college students, we had pooled our pocket money to buy biscuits and tea for rehearsals. We had no costumes that didn't come from raiding our parents' wardrobes, no sets that weren't made from fabric and cardboard. Like children selling raffle tickets for the school fete, we had gone door to door, wheedling money out of people we called 'chachu' and 'dadda' and 'aunty'.

Along with a ripple of nostalgia, I felt a surge of relief. It would be an amateurish venture of course, but it afforded some opportunity for atonement. I texted Asghar, offering to put in an appearance in his play, lend my face and name to the event. He might sell a few more tickets that way. Asghar didn't bother to reply.

The same month, I got busy with an outstation shoot in Mahabaleshwar. It was a short film on a tight budget, which meant three days of non-stop work in rainy weather. There was barely enough time to take a walk around the market and pose for a few selfies with whoever recognized me. In the evenings, I'd sit in my damp hotel room and wonder what was going on in Baansa. Why hadn't Cheeku called with an update? Then I'd tell myself to relax. Nothing was ever really up in Baansa.

A whole week passed before Cheeku called me. He sounded subdued. Aggu, he complained, has changed. He no longer throws himself into things the way he used to. Worse, he refuses to work with students. In fact, he spends all his time in the library, bashing away at his laptop. What kind of theatre is that?

'It's the right thing to do,' I said soothingly. 'Just as well he's being cautious. Go back to your shop, Cheeks. At least one of my friends must remain solvent!'

We laughed together, but the call left me uneasy. What *was* Asghar up to? Nobody in Baansa acted in plays except for students. Grown-ups had grown-up jobs. Almost nobody had the sort of inheritance that would let them take time off for theatre. The handful who did have an inheritance had too much of a sense of dignity to be seen clowning about on stage. These were the sort of people who deigned to attend a show if you went to them with a printed invitation card, bowing and scraping and insisting they grace the occasion. Asghar knew this.

Another month passed before Cheeku called me, nervous excitement spilling down the line. He barely got 'Hello' out of the way before telling me that they were doing *Doctor Faustus*, in Hindi.

'Who'll come to watch *Faust* in Baansa?' Cheeku moaned. 'No romance, no fighting, not even a proper murder.'

I said nothing. The news was a needle-stab in my heart. I had always wanted to play Faustus. Asghar knew this too.

That day on, in every meeting and recording, through all interviews and appearances, the worm of a single thought wiggled about in my head: who would Asghar cast as his Faustus? I made a mental list of our old theatre friends from college. Most of them had left town long ago. Those who had stayed were harried, married, and saving to put their kids through college; quitting jobs to work on a play was out of the question. It would be Asghar himself, I thought. It had to be.

I argued with him inside my own head: *It's a bad idea to cast yourself. You will be needed offstage, especially in Baansa. Besides, Faustus isn't a good-looking man. You want a clever, ambitious, perhaps unattractive actor. He must be able to repel audiences. A thick nose. Too-thin lips. A face that spells out the ugliness of his bargain. In a place like Baansa, audiences need physical aids to their understanding of a character. You know you're not right for it!*

And so on. When I asked Cheeku about what actors they'd found for the play, I was careful to sound laconic. He let out something between a groan and a wail. Asghar was auditioning, would I believe it? He was putting out flyers, calling for actors between twenty-five and forty. Those who wanted to audition were asked to shoot a thirty-second video, reciting a poem in Hindi. The worst of it was that shortlisted candidates were promised reimbursement for bus fare to Baansa and a free lunch afterwards.

'Shakeela ma'am,' Cheeku complained, 'doesn't understand theatre budgets. She wants to feed people.'

I smirked and said, 'Well! It *is* amateur theatre.'

The truth is, travel reimbursement for auditions was an unheard-of luxury. Film producers in Mumbai didn't offer it, regardless of how massive the project was. No theatre group, however professional, had ever offered it to me. Yet, whether or not they could afford it, Act II kept its promise. Bus fares were reimbursed and lunch was served for three consecutive audition days. Mullan was asked to prepare a simple meal of rice, daal, bhindi, and paapad, and she complained bitterly about the louts who ate for two, just because it was free. It didn't help that the gas cylinder ran out on the second day and she had to work on an emergency kerosene stove. If she was to be believed, more than fifty people had auditioned. Sixteen were shortlisted and asked to show up for rehearsals.

My mental argument with Asghar continued. *Too many actors. Bad call. Be sensible. Contemporary directors rework the scenes. Minor characters can be clubbed or edited out.*

I'd seen *Faust* done with just three actors, pre-recorded audio making up for the rest. I'd even seen a German interpretation where there were no actors at all—just anime characters projected on stage alongside a live orchestra. There's so much one could do with technology these days and I longed to tell Asghar that he was out of touch. He'd never been to Berlin, or even to Mumbai. He needed to check out the latest dramatic innovations, check out how the professionals worked. There wasn't even a professional venue in Baansa, so what in hell did he think he could pull off?

But Asghar was keeping his cards close, not

revealing his plans even to Cheeku. He bought a second-hand motorbike to get around. His car was in Lucknow so Zubi could use it though she hardly ever did. She still hadn't found a job, or hadn't even tried. There had been whispered arguments over the phone. Mullan couldn't overhear much but she reported that nowadays Shakeela ma'am was calling Zubi every other day, almost as if she was compensating for her son's silence.

In the meantime, Cheeku was tasked with generating advance publicity for *Dr Baal*. I could hazard a guess as to why Asghar had chosen that title for the play. One night, perhaps it was in the second year of college, we had stayed up late, talking about demons. He wanted to adapt Aristophanes's *Peace*. I worried that the text was too old, too distant from our lives, but Asghar argued that it was old enough to be startlingly fresh, and relatable for local audiences. He would represent war as an aggressive demon, but we had to make sure it didn't resemble any character from local mythology. The demon had to be one that was alien to our ethos. So, we spent hours researching gods and demons from other cultures. Baal had been one of my favourites.

The memory was salt rubbed into a cut. Asghar

remembered, and yet he would not talk to me. Still, I had to admit that the title was a good one. There was a sly ambiguity to 'Baal'. It could signal a demonic figure but, in Hindi, the word also functioned as a truncated form of baalak. Boy. I could feel the wheels of Asghar's mind turning within my own. Faustus was a lost boy, fighting for his soul. He pretended to be world-weary when, really, he hadn't fully experienced the world. He read books but had no wisdom or insight into the universality of his own feelings. On the other hand, 'baal' could also mean hair in Hindi. A title like that confuses and delights. One couldn't tell whether the play was going to be a tragedy or a comedy. But how would he translate Mephistopheles?

I sat on my hands to stop myself from calling Asghar that night. I sipped gin and flicked between TV channels, trying to take my mind off the play. It wasn't even a play yet. It was only a poster, a blue flyer with a line sketch of a stethoscope and the words: '*Dr Baal.* Coming Soon…'

A week passed before I caved in and texted Cheeku: 'How high's the kite?'

It was college code. Every time Asghar began work on a production, the rest of us would exchange wary looks. A bed of real flowers? A silver chariot on a budget of three hundred rupees? An eight-foot giant, a ten-inch fairy? Was he high?

He never was, though. He worked with dolls and voices and cardboard tree-puppets and horses with a silver coat thrown on. He got actors to sit on other actors' shoulders and they were transformed into grooms riding mares. It was kitsch and clunky make-do, and yet, on stage, it worked. This time, though, he seemed to be building up a classier campaign for *Dr Baal*.

Cheeku sent me a photo of the latest publicity material. A midnight-blue background with orange and purple flames licking the edges, and the silhouette of a man with a stethoscope positioned around his head in such a way that it suggested a pair of horns. Underneath, in silver lettering, was the question: 'What's your soul worth?'

Nothing kitsch or make-do about it. This was a limited-edition poster, not meant for bus stops or college notice boards. Only fifty copies were printed on stiff paper and sent to dignitaries around town—doctors, retired professors, bureaucrats. Cheeku stressed the word, dignitaries, with an emphasis on *dig*, which made me wonder if it was going to be a crowd-funded affair. If he thought he could raise capital that way, he was nuts. Local *dig*nitaries expected to be sent free tickets to everything in town.

But no, Cheeku said. Asghar had made it clear from the outset that nobody except family members of the cast and crew would get free tickets.

'Speaking of the cast—' I began and Cheeku quickly said that he had to run. He was taking warm samosas to the rehearsal.

Rehearsal meant the play had already been cast. It would be the first play Asghar directed and produced that I wasn't a part of. I'd have poured myself a stiff drink but I was out of gin. So I practised mindfulness for an hour, then went off to judge an inter-collegiate drama competition. It did nothing to distract me from the worm in my head. Had I been just as awful as a student-actor? Was that why Asghar was refusing to work with students?

That night, I texted Cheeku again. How was the rehearsal? He sent back a thumbs up emoji, but not one word about who the new actors were. If Cheeku wasn't volunteering information, it could only mean that he had been asked not to. So, that was that.

**The Comeback**

It tapers off, I'd been warned. After the first flush of attention, the long-anticipated 'break' doesn't always lead to a steady succession of breaks and paycheques. The phone rang less frequently as the year wound down so that, in the new year, I had no films to shoot, no products to endorse, no plays to act in.

The silence of the phone began to stick in my craw. I started to call some of the people I'd worked with before my big break. Hi-hello, what's up, let's do something together type of calls. Theatre is my *first* love, I declared. Let's do something with a bit of scale, I said. All the things I wanted to say to Asghar, I said to others and their chatter washed over me like a soothing balm.

*Yeah, man! Let's do some cold readings, yeah? Let's plan it. Let's time it. Opening at Lights, eh? Love to, man!*

The Lights Festival of Drama was very competitive.

There wasn't much money but among the prize sponsors was the Priyadarshini Theatre in the heart of Delhi. The winning play would be given the stage free of cost for a month, including the rig and tech assistants, so that the winning production could actually hope to make a bit of profit. Besides, everyone who was anyone on the theatre circuit was either among the participants or in the audience. I fell asleep dreaming of being on that stage, taking a bow, holding a giant bouquet, grinning until tears flowed from my eyes, champagne at the party afterwards, paid for by another sponsor.

When I woke up, I had a sneaky thought about mounting a parallel production of *Dr Faustus*, but then I pushed the thought away. I couldn't sink that low. Still, there had to be another character of equivalent weight that I could sink my teeth into. *Macbeth* was too obvious. *Antigone* had a female lead. Was I too old to play Hamlet? What about Yayati?

I met theatre colleagues at cheap bars to toss about ideas. Tendulkar, Sircar, Karnad were mentioned. The question of where all the women dramatists were came up and was debated until it petered out into the old question of: but isn't gender an artificial construct anyway? The bar swirled with déjà vu. I'd been there, and had had the same conversations before. The only difference was, now younger actors came over to shake my hand. Some of them sat down at my table and looked at me from under their lashes as if my face might drip a honeyed elixir. Even the boys.

It would have been flattering if I'd forgotten the impulses that drive strugglers. I knew that those young actors only came to sit at my table because I still gave off a faint whiff of success. I was there talking to theatre directors and producers, so the table itself was a cynosure. Like me, younger actors wanted to be on stage while they waited for a break in the movies. They knew, as I did, that casting directors kept an eye out for new faces.

'Faces are everything,' I said to them. 'And yet, they're not enough. Voice. Gesture. The thing that lurks beneath the surface of the skin and leaps out only when the director reaches in and snatches it out of you.'

They tilted their heads. They nodded.

'I want to *be*, you know?' I said to Biju, a director for whom I'd done lighting gigs for a decade. 'A text that lets me *be*. Not a text that makes or breaks me. Just *being*.'

Biju nodded. He was a good director but he had just leapt onto the musical bandwagon. Now he wanted to do an original opera, he said, but who could write opera in our context?

'*Con*text!' he stressed, knocking the glass against the table. 'Context is everything.'

Sam, a producer who had only been doing comedies for the last three years, now said that he wanted to work on Brecht.

'Brecht is everything! Everything, man! We should do Brecht together.'

My heart sank. Sam shouldn't do Brecht, I thought, but didn't say. As it turned out, it had only been the vodka talking. He texted me a day later to say that the progressives had beaten all of Brecht's work into a kind of propaganda that was prejudicial to our local audiences, and didn't I agree? I considered responding with an eyeroll emoji, but restrained myself and sent a regular smiley instead.

I scrolled and scrolled down my phone's contact list, not quite knowing who I was looking for until my finger paused at Parul, and at once I understood. It wasn't directors and producers I wanted. I was looking for the old gang. Rakesh, Surya, Parul, Vishnu, Kalyan, Lalit, Cheeku. And of course, Asghar.

What would they think, me calling out of the blue? Me, a legit actor, now that I was doing films and ads that played on television screens across the country. Well, one advert for ginger cookies. Still, I was a minor celebrity and surely it was to my credit that I hadn't forgotten my roots?

I started with Kalyan, who had texted to offer congratulations when the film released. I had forgotten to answer, so I called and offered my apologies.

'It was a crazy time,' I said. 'But I've been missing you all so much. The whole gang! I thought I'd call back after a good night's sleep. Just waking up, I guess.'

Then I asked him about himself. No, he said, he wasn't doing any theatre. No, he hardly ever went back to Baansa. Yes, his parents lived with him. Yes, the kids were fine.

Rakesh was next. He lived in Delhi and we had met a couple of times after college. Again, I had to start with apologies. Sorry for not calling more often. Sorry, couldn't visit after... No, no, divorced... Don't you miss...? But no, Rakesh didn't miss theatre. He didn't even watch plays any more. He and his wife went to satsangs on the weekend.

Surya's phone number had changed, but it didn't matter. Rakesh told me that Surya was now in the restaurant business and had moved to Hyderabad. Vishnu had moved to Agra to help his father-in-law with a garments factory. Parul was chirpily content but her only connection to theatre was attending her kids' school performances. Lalit was the only one who still performed, sort of. He had taken up the tabla and played well enough to offer musical support to drama groups in Delhi. However, he played only on weekends and had no intention of quitting his day job as a medical representative. None of them had been in touch with Asghar and they knew nothing about fresh developments in Baansa.

Short of going back to Baansa and spying on the rehearsals, I had no way of cracking what I'd begun to think of as the 'Faustus' nut. Asghar had built a hard shell of mystery around the production, not letting any member of the cast and crew talk about it to anyone who wasn't in the rehearsal room. Cheeku had strict instructions not to post a single picture on social media. Why did it bother me so much, not knowing who had bagged the main role? But no, that's not true. It wasn't about knowing. It was not *being* Asghar's Faustus that was driving me mad. Luckily, I soon found distraction in the form of a little film festival in New York.

I had been to Germany and France before, mainly on theatre lighting gigs. This was the first time I had been invited to go anywhere in recognition for my acting talent. I wasn't yet a star, not by movie standards, and I hadn't yet won any awards. Still, it was a big deal to have the festival pay for me to travel. I called everyone I knew in the US, and they all invited me to come visit. Chicago, Boston, Austin. I accepted some offers, made ambiguous promises to others, and googled cheap holiday detours.

I'd be travelling for nearly four weeks and I decided that this was going to be a productive trip. I would execute my own little drama project on Instagram by filming myself in unusual locations, reading passages from classical texts. I'd pick out a monologue or a speech, reading it out loud in deserts, forests, gas stations, log cabins, streams. I'd be Hamlet and Claudius and Ophelia, all at once. I'd show them. I'd show *him*.

Eventually, I did make some videos. Three, to be precise. I had the famous Brutus speech from *Julius Caesar* by heart and I did it standing on top of a cliff, pretending to address a tense assembly of backstabbers and turncoats. After that, I did Hamlet's to-be-or-not-to-be soliloquy while standing in the deep end of the hotel's swimming pool. Finally, I did Portia's quality-of-mercy-is-not-strained with the Statue of Liberty for a backdrop. However, I couldn't trek through the desert, or chop wood outside the log cabin, or even soak my feet in a cold stream. There were simply too many parties to attend in New York.

By the end of the month, my Insta readings had attracted only a few hundred views, not the hundreds of thousands that I had been expecting. Scrolling obsessively, I remembered that Zubi was on Instagram too. In the past, she had always commented and liked everything I posted. I went over to her page now to check for updates. There was only one recent post. A photo of a cake she'd baked for her father's birthday, captioned: *Count your blessings*.

I dithered between commenting and not commenting, then decided not to. She was still furious and there was no knowing what she might say to me in public.

After I returned from my American whirlwind, even before I was unpacked, I sent out a flurry of texts to say that I was back in town, and then I waited. But nothing. Not a single call for film work. Neither radio, nor audio. Biju replied to my text saying he wasn't really up for a new production this year. He wanted to keep playing the older shows to recoup some cash, but we'd do some cold readings, yeah?

**The Comeback**

Sam put out a call for a new stage musical, but he only wanted actors between sixteen and twenty-eight. I was already thirty-eight.

I took a long look at myself in the mirror. Fortyish, definitely, although not yet fat or wrinkled. Barrelled torso, short neck, fleshy hands, big nose, little eyes. Who wanted that sort of actor? And yet, I did have something else. A fluid soul, Asghar had said once. A soul that came rising up in my veins, flashing in my face at the right moments.

'I don't know about liquid or solid. Just tell me what to do,' I had said, and Asghar had laughed, clipping me on the side of my head.

'Don't *do* anything. Just *be*.'

That was the year we did *The Comedy of Errors*. Asghar had translated it into Hindi, directed, and choreographed it, and he never hit a false note. The audience, other university students for the most part, had whooped and whistled right through. Afterwards, a Hindi literature professor had come up to shake our hands, and to say that he wished he could have boasted that we were his students. Asghar had been only nineteen then.

When I couldn't take the silence any more, I called Cheeku to ask, 'So, what's it looking like?'

He sighed. Things were not good at Asghar's. There had been more hissing arguments over the phone. Zubi was outright refusing to take up a job. She was being offered entry-level positions that didn't cover the cost of living. If she must go on living with her parents, she said, she may as well accept their care in full and be gracious about it. Asghar tried to argue that it was her duty to ease her father's financial burden. Zubi retorted, saying that it was Asghar's duty to support his family. In frustration, Asghar asked what she'd do if he had died. Would she assume no financial responsibility at all? In that event, she snapped, his opinion about her life choices would no longer matter.

On Eid, Asghar rode his motorbike all the way to Lucknow but he didn't stay the night. After dinner with his in-laws, he rode back, all five hours in the dark. Shakeela ma'am sat near the door, muttering prayers for his safety on the highway. At four in the morning, he stumbled home and asked for an egg sandwich. By the time she had made it and brought it to him, he was fast asleep on the carpet.

The next morning, he sat his mother down and asked if she still thought that he ought to find any kind of job at all so he could send money to Zubi. Selling insurance, garments, toys, cell phones. Shakeela ma'am was silent for a moment, then she asked if that's what Zubi wanted him to do. He shrugged and when he spoke, there was a fleck of bitterness in his voice.

'Amma, marriage is a partnership, is it not?'

'It is. Although both partners may not have the same capabilities.'

'I told her we could pull the girls out of that school in Lucknow, get them educated in Baansa for a couple of years. What's wrong with that? Here, I can feed my family. People live in places like Baansa too, don't they? People grow up here, study here, are buried here. It's not like we're starving or illiterate.'

Shakeela ma'am gestured to Asghar to come closer and she kissed his face.

'Growth is painful, son. Especially when we are asked to grow out of false expectation. It was hard for me too, after your father died. Harder than I'll admit. She will learn in her own time. Don't let your heart harden against her.'

Shakeela ma'am told him to focus on his studies

and on his theatre production. His mother was still alive, she said, and nobody would starve. There was, of course, the question of how much more of her savings she could dip into without having to go back to scrounging for tuitions to make ends meet.

It was at this juncture that Cheeku offered, once again, to finance the play, and once again, Asghar refused.

'Just keep the samosas coming,' he said. 'Also, find me the most beautiful woman in the world.'

Cheeku sputtered. 'In Baansa?'

Asghar grinned. 'And who do you think is the most beautiful woman in the world?'

I could envision Cheeku cocking his head this way and that, trying to guess at the right answer.

'Your mother?'

'From your perspective, you fool!'

'My mother?'

'She's a bit far to make it to rehearsals, no?'

Cheeku's mother had died years ago. I could have told him the right answer at once—his own wife—and after a long detour, Cheeku did arrive at it. His face grew flushed, first with excitement, then with alarm. His wife, Mina, was undoubtedly pretty. She could be persuaded to play Helen of Troy and was only needed on stage for a few seconds, but his extended family would not approve. There would be talk. Cheeku fretted, swinging between yes and no until Asghar told him that the decision wasn't really theirs to make. It should be up to Mina, and Mina jumped at the chance.

The next challenge was the venue. Baansa had only three performance spaces—a covered stage at the degree college, an open-air amphitheatre on the grounds of the government secondary school, and a private hall that was mainly used for wedding receptions and, occasionally, for ghazal nights. But Asghar wanted none of these. He said he needed a stage that would be like putty in his hands. To this end, he hired the old Apsara cinema, near the bus stop. Built in the 1980s, it had already grown derelict when we were undergraduates. Nowadays, it only showed B- and C-grade movies and the few men—only men—who paid for a ticket were either looking for a few hours of respite from the heat or the rain, or else, they needed some external impetus towards masturbation.

Apsara didn't have a stage at all. It had only a raised platform, about six feet wide and thirty feet across, in front of the projection screen. There was no rigging for the lights and nowhere to put the props backstage. It was an awful plan, I protested, but Cheeku disagreed. For a month, the owner of the cinema would allow Asghar to do whatever he wanted with the theatre in exchange for a thorough cleaning, fumigation, and a fresh coat of paint. New vents were being cut into the ceiling, iron cables were being stretched across the width of the hall. The lighting rig would get rigged somehow, but those cables would give them lots of leverage. Banners, bunting, smoke, mirrors—the possibilities were endless.

I asked if Shakeela ma'am had mortgaged her house to allow for such possibilities.

'Why,' asked Cheeku, 'are you shouting?'

A few weeks later, my brother Aun went to visit our parents in Baansa, and I asked him to go check out Apsara. What was it looking like these days?

Aun sent me a photo of a pristine white building that I wouldn't have recognized but for the word 'Apsara' painted in midnight-blue lettering over the entrance. What were the insides like? I asked and Aun said, nobody except the cast and crew were allowed inside the building. I urged him to go in anyway, to take a little peek.

He said, 'Bhai, why don't you come here and take a peek yourself if you care that much?'

For hours, I stared at the photo on my phone, zooming in and out. The theatre, freshly whitewashed, looked striking amid the clutter of food stalls and mobile phone shops on either flank. The blue-tinted whitewash seemed to have swallowed up the grey swill of the gutters, the screaming reds and yellows of the hoardings. Instead of melding with the disarray and gaudiness of the street, the building loomed like a symbol of a genteel past that stood, literally and figuratively, above the market. I could see that the building was, like the drama itself, a sort of public fantasy that Asghar was creating.

Tickets for the play were selling at five hundred rupees. The average movie ticket cost only ninety rupees in Baansa, and at old theatres like Apsara, a matinee ticket cost just thirty rupees. Who would come to watch *Dr Baal* at that price?

Complimentary tickets, as promised, were offered only to the family members of the cast and crew. No bureaucrats, no doctors, no police officials, no professors were invited. Cheeku had tried to argue, these were not the sort of people one could afford to piss off in a small town like Baansa. They were used to being treated as if their shadow falling across the threshold was a special favour bestowed. But Asghar shrugged off all warnings about consequences, saying that whoever wanted to watch the show would either buy tickets or they'd just have to miss the event that was fast becoming the talk of the town.

Cheeku, however, was a little more grounded. He went with folded hands to the offices of the municipal councillor, the district collector, and the superintendent of police, and he pleaded the case for serious entertainment. A play with a moral lesson attached, he stressed. It would soon be available to the town's gentry in the form of *Dr Baal*, but community leaders like themselves must show the way forward. After all, people do spend money on clothes and cars and fireworks even in places like Baansa. Surely, three hundred prominent citizens could afford to buy one ticket, once a year, as a way of encouraging homegrown talent?

The councillor and district collector bought two tickets each. The superintendent of police bought a ticket for his wife, and promised security. Our former professors bought tickets. The chief medical officer bought a ticket. After that, everyone else bought their own tickets, including my own parents. Still, things could hardly be expected to be as uneventful as that.

The night *Dr Baal* opened, a group of young men

showed up in an SUV, waving a katta and demanding tickets to the show. Nobody knows what was said to make them leave, but the policemen posted at the venue stepped up, and somehow, the show went on unmolested. The house was full on the second night too, and on the third day, there was an extra show in the afternoon with college students being offered tickets at one-third the price.

I called my parents that weekend, hemming on about the weather before asking if they had liked the show. Amma said it was a good deal better than nonsense television. Abba asked if I had ever worked on this sort of theatre in Mumbai. My back went up at once. I asked what he meant by 'this sort'. And so he told me.

Asghar's Faustus was a medical doctor who strikes a bargain with the devil in order to conquer time. Dr Baal travels back into the nineteenth century and begins to mess with social reform and freedom fighters. But he does not bring to them better medicine from the future, nor better sanitation, nor even a warning so people shouldn't make the political mistakes that would divide the country. Instead, he takes to making predictions, pretending to have direct access to God. He even travels into the future and twists the course of history by telling people lies about the past. In the end, however, he discovers that he has gained nothing of value, and he no longer knows what to do with his gift of time.

Genius! I wanted to say, but didn't. I could only bring myself to ask my father if people in Baansa understood the subtext.

'No, no, how could they?' Abba snapped. 'People in Baansa put their brains into stamped envelopes and post them to Mumbai every time they want to go out to the theatre.'

At last, I learnt that Faustus had been played by one Sameer Singh. His father owned sixteen acres of land and didn't mind that his second son disappeared into rehearsals for several weeks, especially since it wasn't yet harvest season. I called Cheeku to rail at him. Why all the secrecy?

Cheeku simply laughed. 'And if I had told you, what then?'

What then, indeed? What with having no work in Mumbai and with Asghar shutting me out completely, I had become obsessed with discovering who he had chosen in my stead. Now I searched for 'Sameer + Baansa' on social media and found a page that had shared a poster of *Dr Baal*. Photos revealed a swarthy youth in his mid-twenties. Thin hair, weak jaw, but he could play the flute and make snappy Tiktok videos. In the days following the show, Sameer's display pictures changed. He was now wearing tighter t-shirts and dark glasses, striking typical bumpkin poses—stretching his arms out against waterfalls, leaning against car bonnets. Next thing you know, he'll be taking a train to Mumbai to become a movie star, I thought.

Meanwhile, I stalked, I paced, I sulked. And I twiddled my thumbs. Or rather, I exercised them on my phone. I spent hours hunting down each member of the cast and crew of *Dr Baal*. A month after it opened in Baansa, the play was reviewed in *Rozana* and the Baansa social networks were fired up. The Hindi press rarely covered stage shows even in large cities like Lucknow. Their entertainment pages were devoted entirely to Hindi movies and soaps on television, and their coverage of small towns was restricted to violent crime and the assembly elections. To have a play reviewed by a major newspaper in the Hindi belt was unusual enough, but this was another kind of triumph—a glowing and rather astute review written by someone who had travelled all the way from Lucknow to Baansa specifically for the purpose of watching *Dr Baal*.

The Comeback

The reviewer, K. N. Jha, turned out to be the same Hindi professor who had complimented our undergraduate theatre efforts all those years ago. He had retired since and moved to Lucknow to be closer to his grandchildren, but as soon as he heard that someone had adapted Dr Faustus into Hindi, he promptly boarded a train to Baansa. What he saw compelled him to write a review where he expressed a wish for the show to travel to bigger cities like Agra and Lucknow, for he had not seen anything better on stage in all the seventy years he had lived on earth.

Nobody in the mainstream press cared about theatre as such, but Professor Jha had a nephew who worked for *Rozana*. It had been a slow news weekend and the review filled space nicely on page five of the Lucknow edition. *Dr Baal* was called 'an imaginative, grounded, contextualized, and effectively realized adaptation of one of the greatest dramatic texts in the world…a fresh examination of morality and contracts, humanity and posterity, undeserved power and punishment'. Best thing since sliced bread, basically. Retired Professor Jha then posted a clipping of this published review on social media, wherefrom it was shared further by everyone who had the flimsiest connection with Baansa. Eventually, somebody translated the review into English and it was shared on Instagram by nostalgic alumni who started to tag our old college gang in their posts, me included. At last, a journalist from *Rozana* called me for comment: what did I, the only actor from Baansa to have made it to Bollywood, think about the stupendous success of *Dr Baal*?

Another twist of the knife. I had to confess that I hadn't yet watched the play, but it has been so wonderful hearing such great things about it. Small towns deserve good theatre, I said.

'And what are you busy with these days?' asked the journalist.

'Actually, I hope to return to my first love,' I said. 'I'm going to work in a play.'

Just the week before, QuB, a freelance casting director who worked the Asia scene for West End producers, had called. They had noticed my 'reading' videos on Instagram, and wanted me to audition for Malvolio in a new multicultural production of *Twelfth Night*. I didn't yet know who was producing and I hadn't even auditioned yet but I couldn't resist talking about it, if only in the hope that word would trickle back to Asghar. He still hadn't responded to the text I sent, congratulating him on his marvellous achievement, and the more he treated me like I were spam on his phone, the more desperate I grew to do something to grab his attention.

When the time came, I threw everything at the audition for *Twelfth Night*. I grew out my sideburns. I wore a ridiculous orange t-shirt, two sizes too small so that some of my belly hair showed. I memorized all of Malvolio's lines instead of reading off the page. It paid off and I was shortlisted. However, I was told to knock off five pounds and to limber up because the show might have some rope work. And did I play any kind of drums?

Shortlisted didn't mean cast, but I wanted to call Asghar at once. *Look! Me, on the world stage!*

The producers intended for the show to go around the world with performances in the home country of each of the actors. Assuming I made the cut, I'd be in London, Paris, perhaps even Pretoria! If I were drunk enough, I'd have called Asghar to crow and to rail at midnight, but I wasn't drinking those days. I'd started a keto diet, enrolled in power yoga class, and was also taking dholak lessons. And though the production would pay well once rehearsals began, there was no money for all this prep work. So, once again, I was scrounging: audiobooks, radio jingles, anything that came to hand.

Meanwhile, Asghar was busy studying for his BA first-year exams, and Zubi was trying to make peace with her status as the penniless wife of an artist-student. She did come to watch *Dr Baal* with the children, but then she argued with Asghar about how the show wasn't child-friendly. She was especially incensed when he told Afsana that she could spend the summer holidays in Baansa, helping out with his next production.

'Don't put ideas into her head,' Zubi said. 'She's got to study harder now that she's going into the tenth. She's going to try for medicine.'

'Is that her idea, medicine?' Asghar asked.

'It's Mumma's idea,' Afsana piped up. 'I want to do literature. Or fine arts.'

'Performing arts, maybe?'

If Shakeela ma'am had not asked for a cup of tea just then, the conversation would have taken a very unpleasant turn. As it was, Zubi flounced out of the room and took the children back to Lucknow the very next day. Still, she couldn't protest as vehemently as she would have liked because, to everyone's surprise, the production had not wiped out her mother-in-law's life savings. None of the actors or crew members had been promised more than bus fare for rehearsals and a daily stipend for show days, so they were pleasantly surprised when they were handed a small bonus fee at the end of the first run. Once the accounts were totted up, there was a net loss of just one thousand three hundred and twelve rupees.

Over the summer, Act II raised funds for their next production by offering live home entertainment—poetry recitals, short comic sketches, folk songs. The actors, musicians, and the drama company agreed to split the money equally. This sort of work required very little rehearsal time and it served to keep the newly trained actors on their toes. Over four months, they were hired for three such events and the company earned another four thousand rupees. The books went from red into black and when Cheeku next called, it was to say that Asghar had chosen the text for their next project. It was going to be *The Rover*.

Suspicion, paranoia, self-doubt are alien to me. Still, it was hard to shake off the feeling that Asghar was deliberately picking plays where I would ideally have been cast as lead. Except, I wasn't. Willmore was the sort of character I could inhabit without even trying. It was almost as if Asghar was rubbing my nose in it. Worse, I was eaten up by the thought that I should have produced that play myself. *The Rover*, with its rambunctious themes, its cross-dressing, its endless laughter, was bound to be an instant hit in *any* culture. It just needed a few adaptive touches. Why hadn't I thought of it first?

I kicked myself for days and now it felt even more urgent that I somehow land a role in the multicultural world-touring *Twelfth Night*. For the final round of auditions, the Welsh director Alys would be flying into Mumbai. I had googled her enough to know that she had a thing for ropes, silks, and tap-dancing. So, I had signed up for an aerial yoga class and was practising hanging upside down while shouting out Malvolio's lines. But I still had two kilos to knock off and had gone five weeks without alcohol when QuB texted the date and time for the final audition.

The venue for the audition turned out to be one of those Zumba rooms with mirrored walls on either side. The floor was strewn with a half-dozen props and musical instruments, but no ropes or silks. We were told to use what we could to showcase our musical abilities while we read out the lines we'd be handed. Three other actors had been shortlisted for Malvolio and we were all asked to read the same lines. It was awful, trying not to do what the others were doing and yet, doing the same thing, only a tiny bit better. When it was my turn, I shut my eyes and imagined how I'd play this to an audience that had never heard of *Twelfth Night*. How would Asghar want me to play this?

I reached for a dholak and belched out a snatch of a Dehati folk song I remembered from one of our college shows. The words scarcely mattered, for nobody in the room understood the dialect. *Be,* Asghar would have said, so I tried to simply *be* a Malvolio from Baansa, grinning suggestively before trotting out my lines in a mishmash of English and Dehati.

It was hard to tell what Alys thought. She gave me the usual, polite, *Thanks, you'll hear from us.*

I also noted, resentfully, that for all their fancy Arts Council funding, the production company had not reimbursed commute costs for auditioning actors. Not even bus fare.

The summer stretched all of us to breaking point. I was barely making the rent in Mumbai while in Baansa, Shakeela ma'am suffered a mysterious low-grade fever. Worse, Mina had yet another miscarriage. Cheeku wept quietly beside her and raged loudly over a phone call with me. They hadn't even known she was pregnant and although it was her third miscarriage, this time around, his family blamed it on her going up on stage instead of staying home and being wifely.

Things were hotting up in Lucknow too. I doubted that Zubi would quit the marriage after all these years, but over the last few weeks, her Instagram page had been littered with tiresome homilies about maternal fortitude, cat videos, and short verses by Rumi and Kahlil Gibran. Not one word about her husband's smashing play and its successful reception in Baansa and beyond. It was almost as if she were disowning him.

If Mullan's ears were to be trusted, there had been a massive row over the phone at the start of the girls' summer holidays. Afterwards, Asghar had gone to Lucknow and returned with his daughters. Their school breaks, he insisted, would be spent with their father and paternal grandmother in Baansa.

Zubi tried to argue that the girls needed extra coaching over the summer, especially Afsana, who must start prepping for her board exams.

'No,' Asghar said, and that was that.

Zubi reluctantly packed the girls' things but she did not pack a suitcase for herself. She told Asghar that he should take the car but he declared that the girls were now old enough to negotiate the realities of life. He insisted on bringing them home on a bus.

Zubi's parents were shaken. For fifteen years, Asghar had been a model son-in-law, shielding his wife and daughters from every discomfort. Why should he introduce them to the realities of life now? What next? Were they to drink 'real' water and study in 'real' schools? Two weeks into the summer break, they called Shakeela ma'am to say that they were missing the girls terribly.

'And here I am, missing our Dulhan,' she said amiably. 'Why don't you all drive down and stay for a few days? The air is cooler in Baansa.'

Asghar's in-laws hemmed and hawed for a while, then said that they'd see about finding a driver. They didn't feel confident driving on highways. Bad knees and weak eyes and so on. A few days later, they did come to visit, but Zubi was not with them. Zubi was unwell, they said. She couldn't handle the long road trip, not to mention the heat and the frequent and extended power cuts in Baansa.

Shakeela ma'am told Asghar to go at once and check up on his wife's health. He said he would go but the children would stay put. If Zubi was feeling poorly, he said, she deserved a break from childcare. Besides, the girls were doing just fine, despite the frequent and extended power cuts in Baansa.

The next day, Zubi's parents returned to Lucknow without the girls. While leaving, they gave Afsana and Tarana a large bag of chocolate each, and asked if they'd like to come home. The whole family was going up to the hills for a proper vacation. Their cousins would be coming. Wouldn't they like to go too?

The girls grinned and said no, they were too busy. They were learning to make props for Act II's next production. This revelation led to another heated phone call.

The Comeback

'Have they finished their school projects yet?' Zubi asked.

'They will, when it's time to go back to school,' Asghar said.

'They'll lose touch with studies completely,' she argued.

'It's not a great school if they have to constantly "stay in touch" to learn anything,' he countered.

'Why are you bent on turning them out like this?'

'Like what?'

Zubi stopped short of spelling it out but she had already implied it. Later that evening, Asghar asked his daughters if they'd like to move schools so that they could stay in Baansa year-round.

Tarana looked at her older sister to supply the answer. Afsana stared at her father's face. She was old enough to work out the implications of her mother's absence over the summer. Thankfully, their grandmother stepped in to defuse the moment.

'Don't put such ideas into their heads,' she scolded Asghar. 'They *must* return to Lucknow. And they must finish their school projects. Starting tomorrow, girls!'

At the end of the month, Shakeela ma'am insisted on hiring a car and taking the girls to Lucknow herself. Once she was there, she went out with Zubi to run some more tests to diagnose her mystery fevers. Afterwards, she insisted on going to Hazratganj. To relive memories, she said. She had once gone out on a coffee date with Asghar's father, nearly forty years ago.

The old café had disappeared. In its place stood a swanky glass-front café where a single cup of coffee cost two hundred, and a cookie cost over a hundred rupees. Shakeela ma'am insisted it was her treat, but her hands shook as she opened her purse. Later, as she bit into a cookie, she reported feeling as if she were shredding a hundred-rupee note with her teeth.

'Just sugar and flour, isn't it?' she asked timidly.

Zubi smiled. 'A bit of cocoa, vanilla. Some chocolate chips.'

'Never seen those in Baansa. Are chocolate chips very expensive?'

'Oh, it's daylight robbery, Amma! Everyone knows it doesn't cost that much to make a cookie.'

'Yet everyone pays for it?'

'Everyone who can afford it.'

The question of who could, or couldn't afford to pay for such cookies hung in the air. Both women knew precisely how much they themselves, and the other, could afford.

Nodding at the bustle of the street, Shakeela ma'am

asked, 'You really like this city, don't you?'

Zubi shrugged. 'I'm used to it.'

'One does get used to a particular way of living. There's no right and wrong about it. Everyone craves the familiar. We don't want to let go of what we have, and yet, change is the only constant. No?'

The older woman paused, reached out across the table and took Zubi's hand between her own.

'Listen, child. Cities don't disappear when you leave them. But there are certain places, if you abandon them for too long, they simply crumble into the dust. And one day, when you turn around to look for them...'

Zubi didn't say a word but tears gathered in her eyes and she brushed them away as quickly as they fell. She had understood the danger her mother-in-law hinted at. Shakeela ma'am patted her hands and sighed deeply.

'I better eat every crumb of this biscuit. It's worth, what, half a day's wages for breaking stones in the quarries? But I have to say, Dulhan, if I must pay so much for one little morsel, I'd much rather it were a proper nankhatai or a meethi tikiya.'

And Zubi chuckled through her tears. She said nothing at the time but an idea had been triggered by her mother-in-law's comment. As soon as the girls' school term started, she went to work. Her Instagram page showed off a cane basket piled high with nankhatai. Awadhi cookies, she called them, and they were now available in chocolate, cardamom, pistachio, and apple flavours: fifty-nine rupees per cookie, packaging and shipping extra. Discounts were available on bulk and repeat orders.

The monsoon brought good news. QuB called to say that Malvolio was mine. The first thing I did was to place an order for four hundred Awadhi cookies, one hundred of each flavour. At first, I wondered if Zubi would even accept the order, seeing that it came from my phone number. There was no response for a whole day but the next morning, she messaged back to ask who would be picking up the order.

I had not planned on going to Lucknow but Baansa didn't have an airport. I hadn't even planned on going to Baansa really, but now felt like a good time to visit. I hadn't been home since my big movie outing and my parents no longer visited me in Mumbai. They weren't thrilled when I married Sejal, but they had come around. However, Sejal leaving me—especially after they discovered why she left—had been the last straw. They stopped visiting and they stopped asking me any questions about where I lived, with whom, and whether or not I was making a decent living.

It had been a very long time since my parents had been proud of me. They hadn't been happy when I insisted on studying acting instead of doing an MBA. Still, in the early years, they were not overly worried. I was living in Mumbai with Qaiser Mamoo, my mother's cousin, and he had promised to keep an eye on me. This meant he would save me from the smoking, drinking, drugging, sex dens of iniquity that was the world of movies. My parents had thought I'd take my chances, fail, then settle into some kind of regular work, just like Mamoo did.

In his time, Qaiser Mamoo had wanted to be a playback singer in the movies. After a few years of knocking about, he had settled into a steady dribble of work as a sound engineer in a recording studio. He made enough to marry and look after a family and nobody could point a finger at him or call him disreputable. He smoked his share of cigarettes and even though he cautioned me about the pitted road to stardom, he was too fond of me to belabour the point. Besides, his daughter Nazo and I were very fond of each other.

Nazo had first visited Baansa when we were both about eight. It didn't take long for us to fall into what

I thought of as friendship, and which she had assumed was the promise of family. Sadaf Mumaani was already quite sick by the time I arrived in Mumbai, so it was Nazo who cooked, Nazo who waited up for me, and warmed up my dinner when I came home late. It was Nazo who repaired my shirts, Nazo who listened to my stories about acting school and who laughed at every anecdote. It was Nazo who waited. And waited.

They would have started looking for potential grooms years ago, but when Qaiser Mamoo and Sadaf Mumaani saw us laughing together, they had assumed that there was no need to look further than home. In two years, I had my acting diploma and yet, I stayed on in their cramped two-bed flat. I paid no rent, did no chores. Nobody said a word about what was expected of me. There was one expectation only, and it went unvoiced.

My own parents would sometimes ask, with a teasing inflection in their voices, how Nazo was doing, so I must have known what was expected. But I had other plans, other interests. First, there was Avantika from my acting class, although I was careful not to mention her at home. She didn't mention me at her home either. It was one of those things we both knew was temporary. Then, when I began to find work tackling lighting rigs at a theatre company, I met Sejal. She was a writer, three years older, and with a bracing wit that disarmed even when it cut close to the bone. I was invited to a few of her house parties and each time, I stayed later and later.

I knew then that I wasn't going to marry Nazo and yet, I didn't leave my uncle's household. Not until I had landed my first acting role, a bit part in an ensemble film. Soon after, I rented a single room with a kitchenette. But I told my family that the room was in a ghastly building, full of jobless louts and possibly, junkies too. I couldn't possibly have anyone else living there with me.

Nazo waited another year, but I was visiting Qaiser Mamoo much less frequently. When I did visit, I had fewer stories to share with her. Over that year, I saw her smiles fading into lines of pain. The next year, Sejal and I moved in together. The year after that, we were married at the registrar's. Aun showed up as a witness, but nobody else from the family. Six months later, my parents relented and hosted a small reception for us in Baansa. Qaiser Mamoo and Nazo did not attend, citing Sadaf Mumaani's health.

Despite the expense of it, Sejal and I rented a flat with a spare bedroom. She said all the right things about how we had to have a family room, one that was always waiting to be occupied. Once a year, my parents would visit and they stayed about a month. They learnt to be satisfied if they got to watch a play or a film that either of us was involved with. We hosted parties where almost everyone invited was an actor, a writer or theatre-maker. Aun was in college by then, and he came to visit us a few times a year. In this way, four years passed.

Sejal had two root canals done. I had my wisdom teeth removed. Neither of us talked about children because we knew what our bank statements looked like. But there was more to it than money. There was a black hole in our marriage that neither of us wanted to acknowledge. It was in the way Sejal would look at me when we were alone, the weight of silence pressing down on us. The way I found myself delaying my return home after a long day of work, going out for a drink with friends instead. The way I told stories about my work and Sejal didn't laugh. Instead, she would frown and pick at each bit of gossip for hidden meaning, as if she were intent on grasping a shift in industry loyalties and the formation of new cliques. She wasn't that intent on how I felt.

Then came the day I bumped into Avantika at an

audition. It was just one of those things—an audition fling, she called it—but I let Sejal know what had happened. I didn't have to, but I said that I wanted complete honesty between us.

Sejal said, 'Fuck you, John! You're crap at honesty.'

She stuck around for a few weeks but then said that if we're being honest, it's best that we move into separate apartments for a while. I knew it wouldn't be 'for a while'. She needed to live apart from me for six months before she could take the next legal step, but I didn't argue. Six months later, Sejal filed for divorce.

During that separation phase, I had visited Lucknow and stayed with Asghar and Zubi for a few weeks. I had ranted about how nobody understood me—not my parents, not Nazo, not Sejal. Just like I had ranted before about the awful family pressure to tie me down to the nearest post and to saddle me with responsibilities before my career had a chance to take off. I had ranted and ranted about the double bind of honesty and familial hypocrisy, and Asghar quietly listened.

The day I was set to return to Mumbai, he had gifted me a photo of myself, blown up to poster size. It was from when I was eighteen. I was skinny then, and dressed in a white kurta that the rain had made utterly transparent. If I wasn't beautiful, I was at least vulnerable and unselfconscious.

'A new companion for your bedroom,' he joked. 'Make sure this one is for keeps.'

At the time, Asghar and Zubi kept a neat home in Lucknow with airy balconies filled with pots of jasmine, roses, and lemongrass. When I'd last visited them, the girls were old enough to take an interest in movie gossip and they asked dozens of questions about who among the famous film stars I had met. Zubi would make omelettes and parathas for breakfast, and kebab-roti for dinner. I couldn't drink inside the house but Asghar would slip away with me now and then to the rooftop where we would talk half the night. Me, nursing a gin and tonic, and him, just the tonic. But of course, Asghar would have had to let go of that beautiful house. This time, I was headed to a different address—Zubi's parents' house, where the garden was much bigger and my reception much colder.

It was Zubi's father who answered the door. He had my package of Awadhi cookies wrapped up and ready in its basket, and he tried to fob me off at the doorstep. I grinned and offered a salam, addressed him as 'uncle' and asked where Zubi was. I said how great it was that she was putting her talent to use at last.

**The Comeback**

I peered over his shoulder and caught a glimpse of Tarana. Still in her school uniform, she was peeking out at me from behind a curtain. I called out to her but she promptly disappeared into an inner room.

Zubi's father was too polite to yell at me but he held his ground, not inviting me in. His eyes darted about uneasily, as if he was speaking to a notorious convict rather than an actor with whom he'd once insisted on taking a selfie. A spark of anger flared up in my belly. I called Zubi's phone right then and demanded to know if she wouldn't even see me, after I'd come all this way. As if I still had the right to say such things.

She met me in 'Ganj, at the same coffee shop where she'd taken her mother-in-law and found inspiration for her new baking business. I complimented her cookies and that's when she told me the story. Her eyes were wary, though, and at last, she spat it out.

'You're too much, you know? Just showing up here as if... What do you want?'

I put my head in my hands. I rubbed my eyes. I folded my hands before her.

'The last thing I want—'

'What you want is irrelevant anyway. I don't care. Asghar doesn't care either. The only reason I'm meeting you here is that I don't want you upsetting my parents in their own home.'

'Really? Then you should have told me to get lost over the phone. Come on, Zubi! We—you and I—we've known each other fifteen years. Asghar and I have been best friends since we were seventeen! One doesn't just quit a friendship like that.'

'You know what, Jaun?' And she drew out the 'au' in my name like it were a brick she was throwing at my face. 'The problem is not quitting a friendship. The problem is, you don't know how to stand up for a friend. Even if I did care, and even if Asghar cared, the truth is that you don't care about us.'

'Zubi–' I started to protest but she wouldn't let me get a word in.

'You don't care about anyone or anything except your stupid ambition to be in films. You didn't care about your parents and who would look after them. You married Sejal, and you didn't care about what would happen to Nazo. And ultimately, you didn't care about Sejal either.'

'Wait a minute. Sejal was bored sick. She *wanted* to leave. I just supplied her with an acceptable excuse. And we're still friends, you know. In fact, she's keeping my stuff while I travel—'

The Comeback

'Of course she is! Are you still "friends" with that other girl too?'

'Who? Look, *she* was the one who came on to me.'

'And how many affairs since? Four, five? A new woman every month?'

'That's really unfair, Zubi.'

'Don't talk to me about unfair, Jaun. You know what your philandering means? It means you don't care. You think you know how I'm feeling? Gossip travels, no? You must have heard we've been fighting. You can't get through to Asghar, so you're trying to cosy up to me. You think I need someone to talk to because I'm mad at my husband. You'll say two sympathetic words and I'll pour out all my rage, cry on your shoulder.'

'Zubi—'

'And once you and I are friendly again, you imagine that Asghar will have no option but to embrace you again. He's always been generous, hasn't he? So he'll give you your forgiveness in the end. That's the plan, yes?'

I threw up my hands in protest, but there was nothing left for me to say. Zubi swallowed her coffee in one bitter mouthful.

'He might forgive you, Jaun, but I swear to God,

it won't be on my account. You want forgiveness? Earn it! For once, deserve something!'

'You're angry, Zubi, and that's fair enough. But I have earned whatever little I have.'

'And precious little it is! One outing on the big screen after seventeen years of running about like a headless chicken. Big deal! It was a mediocre film, by the way. If you can throw your best friend under the bus for *that*, what wouldn't you do for something really big?'

Just as well that she stalked off before I could come up with an appropriate riposte, because I didn't really have one.

The Comeback

My reception in Baansa wasn't especially warm. Amma was saying her prayers more often now, and when I said that I'd be off travelling the world for a few months, she just sighed. Abba asked if those people, meaning the show's international producers, would support my stay in London, because, surely, I wouldn't be paid enough to rent my own place? I tried to persuade Aun to visit home while I was there, but he was too busy.

Cheeku was the only one who met me with any enthusiasm. He came over with a dozen samosas and jalebis, hugged me warmly and marvelled at how much weight I'd lost. He wanted to know all about how I landed this new gig although I'd already told him over the phone.

'Tell me again. Nonono, show me! Show me how you auditioned.'

It was good for my punctured self-image, so I humoured him. Cheeku laughed and clapped, took dozens of photos, and even helped me make new videos for Instagram. There I was, lounging in my old bedroom in a tattered brown sweater, and riding a wobbly old bicycle around the old campus, and posing on the old concrete stage outside college with the hashtag #ThisIsWhereItAllStarted. We visited the bamboo groves that gave the town its name, walked around the bend of the river, shared a sly smoke up on the terrace, hashtag #StillAfraidOfMom.

At every turn, the spectre of Asghar hung in the air and dampened my mood. I should have liked to be at his place, lolling on the takht for hours. We'd take each line in *Twelfth Night* apart. Or rather, he'd take it apart for me, showing me five different ways to approach a line, trying inflection upon inflection until something clicked. I had texted to let him know that I was in town, in case he'd like to meet, but as usual, there was no response.

Cheeku tried to cook up little white lies to make me feel better about Asghar's pointed refusal to meet me.

'He's busy, you know? Trying some new experiment to raise money. I think it's unnecessary but who can stop him? It's his time and his energy.'

He tried to compensate by taking me into Apsara, jabbering endlessly about the lighting and smoke effects used to create visions of devilry and magical time-jumps in *Dr Baal*. He pointed out how the cinema projector and screen had been improvised to make up for the lack of a rig. There were no bars, no booms, no profiles, no fresnels.

'We used wooden screens, LEDs, and a few hanging lanterns. The rest was all shadow-work and paper cut-outs. Projections of backdrops. Asghar said he got the idea from the shadow-work they do with leather puppets in Java.'

The cinema had been a clever choice of venue after all, I could see that now. It was already equipped with dim lights and projection equipment. But when and how did Asghar learn the tricks of Indonesian theatre? I coaxed more information out of Cheeku and it came out in bits and pieces.

Asghar had spent a whole year diversifying his bouquet of skills. He spent hours on YouTube, watching recordings of shows and listening to interviews with the best lighting and sound technicians. Then he'd try out some of those tricks at home. In fact, he was getting rather good at it. He had even been approached by his old high school. They wanted him to come in and add a few 'tricks' to the annual student production, but they weren't willing to pay him. They expected him to feel honoured to have been asked at all.

Asghar refused politely, saying that he was only a student himself and not a magician who could show off any tricks. However, this exchange did alert him to the fact that there were people in Baansa who needed interventions that could only come from drama. Soon he was offering diction and speech classes for a small fee. Thus far, he had only three pupils, all of them young men who wanted to speak Hindi more clearly and to learn how to throw their voice without the aid of a microphone. Cheeku figured they had an eye on politics rather than the stage, but they were fee-paying pupils and the money meant that Asghar could pay for the fuel in his motorbike.

When there was only a week left for me to head back, I began to call the old college gang—Parul, Vishnu, Kalyan, Lalit, Rakesh. I pressed them to travel to Baansa for New Year's Eve. We could have a grand party, a drama club reunion, what say? If they all came, Asghar could not refuse to show up to the party. I would find a way to smooth things over, I thought. But even though everybody said they loved the idea, ultimately, they all had plans with their own families. I would have to spend New Year's Eve watching television with my parents, and leave town without meeting the one person I wanted to meet.

On the morning of the day I was due to leave, I decided to take one last chance. I went over to Shakeela ma'am's house, round to the back lane where his bedroom faced. The window stood open and I peeped in, thinking I'd say 'boo!' Something silly like that. Perhaps he'd snap his head upwards and once he saw my face, my eyes, he'd have to relent. How could he not? But the room was empty and when I mustered up the courage to go around to the front, it was Mullan who answered the door. Bhaiyya wasn't in, she said. Did I want to speak to his mother instead?

I came away, tail between my legs. It was one thing to try and bluster my way back into Asghar's life, even throw myself dramatically at his feet; it was quite another thing to face Shakeela ma'am. Knowing what she had done to her own son for cheating in an exam, I didn't want to know what form her disapproval of me would take.

As I got back on my wobbly bike, I heard Mullan calling out, 'Is it about tuition for the kids? Or did you come for an audition? Don't think you'll get your bus ticket money, now that I've seen you come here riding a cycle.'





The Comeback

London was hard. We arrived in January and nothing about the city felt right. Not the weather, not the food, not the house I had to share with four other actors. I sniffled all the time. My knuckles felt stiff every morning and when I warmed up a dish in the microwave, by the time I'd brought it to the dining table, it was cold again. My mother does a better stew, I complained to my fellow actors when we went out to eat. And the less said about the English style of making tea, the better. As for the biscuits they brought in for the tea breaks, give me an 'Awadhi cookie' any day.

I was also grumpy on account of my score with the ladies. Contrary to Zubi's opinion of me, there wasn't a new woman in my life every month. Since my divorce, there had been only two brief, very dissatisfactory flings with fellow actors, and one affair with a scholar from Australia who was researching postcolonial drama in Mumbai. She had spent the better part of our three-month-long dalliance trying to explain postcolonial, postmodern, and even posthuman theories, and I was frankly relieved when she said she had to return to university. Of course, we'd keep in touch, she said, and so on. We both knew she wouldn't come back. That had been two years ago and nobody else afterwards. I was looking forward to some change in this regard and had mugged up some romantic poetry in anticipation but, God knows for what reason, all the women working on this show were utterly unmoved. Poetry elicited a polite 'wow'. Looking deep into their eyes elicited self-conscious giggles. Ask a woman if she'd like to go out for a drink, she calls the whole gang to come join us.

Rehearsals too were a cold, joyless experience. Alys didn't make me do any ropes or singing, but she did ask me to play the dholak as a background beat for Cesario and Olivia. They were asked to sing a few lines of a duet from an old Hindi film. I tried to argue that it made no sense for my character to provide the background score to their romance, but Alys had her own ideas about rejuvenating the classics. She had cast for a bearded black Sebastian, while Viola was a blue-eyed blonde. There was another black actor in the mix and I didn't see why the two black actors couldn't have played twins. Instead, the sole black female actor was cast to play the fool, Feste.

To me, this felt less like rejuvenation and more like hodgepodge, but I kept my opinions to myself and focussed on being a good Malvolio. The hours were long and even though we were being paid, it wasn't the sort of money one could go partying on. Calling home just added to my misery. My parents rarely had much to say to me, but they did let me know that there was a strong buzz building about Act II's second production.

I couldn't stop thinking about how much more fun it would have been to be in *The Rover*, to be back in Baansa and being directed by Asghar. Then came the shocker: Willmore was yet to be cast but Ned Blunt had been found. It was going to be Cheeku! He told me himself, blushing so fiercely that I could see it on Facetime.

I made the right congratulatory noises, of course, but I was secretly pleased to learn that things were much more difficult for Asghar this time. No female actors could be found to play the four love-hungry ladies. Cheeku's wife was pregnant again and had been advised complete bed-rest. A couple of girls did show up to audition but they couldn't promise that their families would allow them to actually go up on stage. They couldn't be seen chasing men, not even as make-believe, and besides, none of them wanted to play a courtesan. For once, I thought, Asghar would confront the limitations of working in his own milieu. Talent alone doesn't cut it.

February turned to March and Baansa's *The Rover* remained un-cast. There were four rounds of auditions, half a dozen readings, dramatic exercises about throwing voice in an amphitheatre, but still no rehearsals. Cheeku began to sound glum. At this rate, there would be no play and he'd never get to be on stage. Then Asghar got busy with his BA second-year exams and there were no further updates.

Meanwhile, the weather had improved in London but the rehearsal room was colder than ever. Alys looked nervous and rarely smiled. The actor playing Viola had started to disagree violently about the intentionality of her movement, but the movement director had landed another, better-paying gig in Germany and they would not give us any more time. Another actor was threatening to quit, saying that his nerves were frayed and his stomach had been ruined by too much rocket-leaf salad. He had to be mollified with a two-day break in the rehearsal schedule and the option of satay for lunch.

I was on edge too, worried that my absence from the Mumbai film scene would mean losing out on movie projects. Not that anyone was offering me any new work. Still, I spent my lunch break obsessively texting casting directors and sending them 'new look' pictures that they hadn't asked to see. I posted about five times a day on Insta and once, when I bungled a line in rehearsal, Alys made a snide remark about giving actual work a smidgen more attention than pictures of work.

At once, I put my phone away and never took another picture during work hours. Still, I reminded myself not to take Alys's words to heart. It just meant that she was keeping an eye on me, following me on Insta. Besides, I wasn't really forgetting my lines. The only reason I had bungled that line was that my mind was drifting and I was channelling Captain Willmore rather than Malvolio. In a sneaky little corner of my heart, I was still thinking of a way to get a foot in *that* door.

*Twelfth Night* would begin touring the weekend after Easter. If Asghar still hadn't found his Willmore by the time the tour ended, I was determined to throw off the last vestiges of my dignity and grovel at his feet. It would mean not making any money, perhaps for a whole year, but I was willing to pay any price to work with Asghar again. That desire was like bacteria in my gut. I had to fight it so as not to be felled by it, but it was also the same thought that drove me to ace my act.

Our multiracial, multilingual *Twelfth Night* opened at The Globe in London. We went to Paris next, then Rabat, Lagos, Pretoria, Austin, Singapore. Spring dissolved into a whirlwind of airports and hotel check-ins. Just enough time to eat, sleep, warm up, rehearse, and then it was call time. Before and after each show, we were photographed in our multicultural costumes. In each city, Alys and the local actor were interviewed quite intensely and I couldn't wait for when it was my turn in Delhi. In the meantime, two international reviews had already mentioned my turn as Malvolio.

One reviewer particularly noted my clever use of 'comedic light' to steal the show. The review said that the actor's experience in stage-lighting had given him a clear advantage, for he knew the tricks of putting his face forward, angling it towards the warmer spots of light while casting the rest of his body into a subtle shadow. Only someone who knows the tragic and comedic effects of light can achieve this, the reviewer wrote, and of course, it was true. I did know how to do this. The other actors seemed a bit cooler towards me after the review appeared but it would take a lot more than that to faze me. I highlighted all mentions of myself in the international press and kept my Insta lit.

As soon as the plane landed in Delhi, my phone began to ring. Congratulations were already pouring in. Everyone was calling or texting to ask about tickets. That is, everyone except Asghar. I had already sent complimentary tickets for my own family, and now I bought two extra tickets and sent them to Cheeku with the hope that he could persuade our mutual friend to come along. I should have known better.

Cheeku did get on a train and travelled twelve hours to watch the show, but when he came backstage, he was not with Asghar. Instead, he was accompanied by the good Professor Jha, who placed a hand on my head by way of blessing and assured me that he would write a review in *Rozana*. As for Cheeku, he didn't say much more than, 'Best, bro! Best!' But he was playing escort to the professor, he said, and couldn't stay to chat. Eyes shining, he gave me a thumbs-up and disappeared.

My parents also travelled to Delhi to watch the show but they turned down my offer of checking into a hotel room. They stayed at Aun's place in Noida, and that's where I went too, once the production stopped paying for the hotel. Another week passed in a comfortable haze of magazine interviews and complimentary messages. Once the buzz began to fade, my gut began to bother me and I texted Cheeku: 'How high's the kite?'

Uncharacteristically, it took Cheeku a whole day to read my text. When he did reply, it was only to say that it had been mad. He was rehearsing late into the night.

Rehearsal? The high of my own successful tour drained out of my body like water out of a sieve. I wanted to grab Cheeku, drag him right out of the phone, and shake every detail out of his tubby frame. But he really did sound tired and when he began to talk about the difficulties of memorizing lines, I thought I would burst with envy.

I paced Aun's sunny balcony all day, thinking of what to do next. At last, I texted Lalit. He had come to watch *Twelfth Night*, showed his face backstage

The Comeback

for a moment before melting away into the crowd. I now asked him to come out and have a proper drink with me.

When we met, I took the lead in dissing my multicultural show as a lot of hot air.

'It's no good, Lalit. You know it too.'

'But I quite enjoyed the show.'

'Oh, we all *enjoyed* it. We enjoyed our college theatre antics too. But what does that mean?'

Lalit smiled into his drink. I egged him on.

'No, go on, say it. Be honest.'

'Our college stuff wasn't bad. Tacky maybe, but at the heart of it, it was good drama.'

'Unlike the great international production of last week, eh?'

'Jaun, that's not what I meant.'

I threw up my hands. 'Hey! I'm the first to admit it. This was just a "show". Three lines of Hindi, two lines of Chinese, a dholak, a dafli, a violin, some hijinks. Anyway, they liked it in London. Not so much in Lagos.'

Lalit slapped my back sympathetically and offered to buy the next round.

'Now can you imagine,' I went on, 'what someone like Asghar would do with that kind of money?'

'Ah! Well! You never know. He's doing his own experiments. Risky, I feel. Much riskier than this multicultural experiment of yours. Just not as expensive.'

'Really? I haven't been able to catch up lately. What's he up to now?'

'He's doing a gender bender. Going back to old theatre traditions, he claims.'

'What tradition?'

But I didn't need Lalit to answer the question. In a flash of intuition, I knew that Asghar was getting male actors to play women because he simply couldn't find any female actors. As experiments go, it wasn't a very bold move, given that he was doing it for much the same reasons as folks did in the nineteenth century, and I said as much.

'But it's a real risk,' Lalit insisted.

'What risk?'

'It will appear more nautanki than natak, no? Nobody will take it seriously.'

'It's *The Rover*, Lalit!' I said. 'It's not a serious play.'

'I haven't read the script,' Lalit admitted. 'But, yaar, this man is too much. You know K. P. from the Academy? He's handling grassroots development at the Ministry of Culture. He hears about a new director from Baansa doing clever local adaptations, so he invites Asghar to come to Delhi. To give him a break, you know? Guess what our Aggu does? He asks, "What's your budget?" Can you believe it? He wanted the Academy to pay his company to bring his show to Delhi. And when K. P. explains, it's an opportunity for *you*, personally, then Asghar comes back with: "Where's the opportunity in it? Travelling to Delhi is a chore, not an opportunity. Unless you're offering me a full-time job." Unbelievable! And now, what, he's doing a sex comedy?'

My brain had snagged on the words 'Academy' and 'Ministry of Culture'; I paid no attention to the rest. So, Asghar's work was attracting notice in the national capital. As far as stagecraft goes, he couldn't go wrong. But surely, he would need good actors if his play wasn't to descend into a farce?

'I wonder,' I said, 'if he's still looking for rough diamonds in Baansa?'

Lalit laughed and said, 'He did find you, didn't he?'

I dilly-dallied at Aun's place in Noida until the family began to suspect that I was in serious financial trouble. Abba asked if I was staying on because I didn't have a place of my own in Mumbai. Amma asked if the London people had paid me yet. Aun asked whether, after my world tour, I had grown sick of the material world and planned on becoming a jogi.

Something like that, I said to each of them. And when my parents decided to return home, I offered to accompany them. Their train was scheduled to arrive at Baansa a little past midnight. It wasn't safe, I said, not for an elderly couple.

I'd already tried to persuade my parents to hire a taxi instead of rattling about in a train, but Abba's eyebrows reached his hairline. Amma opened her mouth, then thought better of it, but I knew from the way she pursed her lips that she thought me profligate and irresponsible. Aun knew better than to ask: *since when have you started worrying about our parents?* I had rarely dropped them off at the airport when they used to visit me in Mumbai. Instead, he quietly pointed out that it was a ten-hour drive and about half of it would be on roads so bad, there was a serious risk of spinal damage. Ergo, not for an elderly couple.

So the taxi idea was shot down as a foolish waste of money, and inconvenient besides. An extra train ticket was procured for me and, for about twelve hours, I played the ideal son. Bringing my parents tea or soup every hour, making innocuous comments about the scenery outside the window, murmuring darkly about the air-conditioning being too cold and the blankets unwashed, just as well we wouldn't be using the bedding.

Nobody recognized me on the train but when I got off at Kanpur station, a college kid came up at the poori–subzi stall. He took a selfie with oily fingers and then promptly called his mates, who also wanted pictures with me. When the group slowly expanded to include other passengers, I began to take a few selfies too. The students expressed wonder that I still travelled by train, and asked whether it was first class or second. When I said, third AC, they were dumbstruck and wanted yet another round of selfies. I very nearly missed my train and spilled half the subzi while making a run for it. All of it went up as part of my #NeverForgetYourRoots series of posts on Insta.

I felt rather smug at the end of the journey because, just as I had predicted, Baansa was quite unpleasant after midnight. The taxi and autorickshaw drivers lined up outside the railway station were belligerent, and asking for twice the regular rate. My father was losing his cool. My mother looked resigned but was clearly exhausted. She didn't want to have to hang about at the station until dawn. Peering around the taxi stand, I spotted a face I recognized from college, and waved him over enthusiastically. I threw our bags into the boot of his cab without haggling about the price, and my parents were relieved. Not that it stopped them muttering about how the world was no longer fit for honest folk.

Visiting Baansa felt different this time. It was peak summer and the sun was pitiless. The power cuts were long and debilitating. Cheeku wasn't free to hang out with me. He was either busy in rehearsals or spending time at home with his wife. The doctor had mentioned the words 'bed-rest' and 'complication' so often, they were considering moving to Lucknow for a few months and having the baby delivered at a bigger, more expensive hospital.

I finally caught up with Cheeku at the sweet shop early one morning. He met me warmly but when I asked him to show me how he was planning to play his Ned Blunt, he grew evasive. Nor would he tell me who had been cast as Willmore, and whether the text would be played as a Western farce or if it had been adapted nautanki-style. He kept saying, 'God alone knows what it will turn out to be!'

Then, he gave me an unexpected rush of hope. In an effort to cheer me up, he told me that Asghar had liked my turn as Malvolio even if he hadn't liked the show overall.

'Asghar? Really? How? When? Did you secretly film the show?'

'Don't be mad!' Cheeku protested. 'Filming wasn't allowed. Why would I do something like that?'

But his face betrayed him. I could tell that he had let slip something that he wasn't supposed to.

'Cheeku! He came to watch? Come on, what's to hide? You can't keep that from me.'

And so it came out that Asghar too had travelled to Delhi to watch my play. However, he refused to come backstage with Cheeku, and he would not accept a complimentary ticket. He bought a ticket for himself and gruffly said that he was only going because he wanted to see what an international, multicultural, multilingual theatrical adaptation of a Western classic looks like.

'We can do better,' was the only comment he offered after watching the show. Still, when Cheeku went on and on about how great our Jaun had been, Asghar had tilted his head sideways. This means, Cheeku assured me, that he didn't disagree. I *was* actually great.

I was torn between feeling chuffed and feeling weepy. That Cheeku should be interpreting for me the gestures of my own best friend! I had no other 'best' friend for all of my adult life. Even now, apart from Sejal, I didn't really have any other close friends. Tears sprang to my eyes now and Cheeku looked alarmed. He put an arm around my shoulder and promptly asked Bittu to fetch me a cold drink.

'Aggu is just... You know him, right? But he's not... He's got such a big heart. See, he did go to Delhi. He was there on your big day, right? That's what matters... Arre! You can't be like this now.'

Cheeku carried on with his giddy comforting until I stopped him short.

The Comeback

'Let me meet him. Let me fall at his feet and ask forgiveness properly.'

'Yaaaar… Don't. Don't ask—'

'Just tell me where to find him. I won't ask for more, I promise. Cheeku, just this one thing. Tell me how to meet him.'

The next day, I waited outside Apsara theatre a few minutes before noon. A hand-painted sign outside the ticket window said that any show would be cancelled if there were fewer than thirty viewers. The only people who bought matinee tickets in Baansa were either young couples who needed a bit of time in a relatively safe room, or autorickshaw drivers and travelling salesmen who needed a few hours of respite from the blinding summer heat. Afternoon temperatures were touching 46 degrees in the shade but all movie halls had to sell at least thirty tickets to recover the cost of air conditioning. Since Apsara rarely managed those numbers on weekday afternoons, the owner had allowed Act II to use it as rehearsal space at a discounted rate of a hundred rupees an hour, minus the aircon.

At half past twelve, the actors began to trickle out of the building. They emerged in twos and threes, blinking in the harsh sunlight, their clothes damp with sweat. Except for Cheeku, all the faces looked unfamiliar. I waited in the shadows until, at last, Asghar stepped out of the building. He was trailed by an actor I recognized from photos, Sameer Singh, and right behind him, another familiar face. But how? Impossible! Nazo?

My retreat was involuntary. I stepped back into the shadow of the ticket counter and turned my back until the group had disappeared from view. The male actors walked towards the bus stop while Nazo waited in the parking lot. Asghar brought his bike around and then they left, Nazo riding pillion.

Nazo! Here? With Asghar? I was too numb to work it all out and I didn't feel like going home just then. I decided to buy thirty tickets at Apsara and insisted that they run the air-conditioning and screen a movie just for me. The only print they had was *Pyar se Pyara* from the 1990s. I sat in the theatre alone for two and a half hours, not really watching, just trying not to think about what I had seen outside. There wasn't a single good scene in the movie. The colours and sound gave me a headache but it did serve to overcome the storm rising in my chest.

The sun was still intense when I emerged from the theatre. I had spent all the cash I was carrying on the movie tickets, and none of the autorickshaws on the street would accept digital payments. I decided to walk the two kilometres back home. When I arrived, red-faced and bathed in sweat, Amma yelled at me for the first time in a decade. By the time I had showered and changed into pyjamas, I was running a temperature of 104.2.

The heat stroke knocked me out for four days. It hurt to open my eyes and I could sit up just long enough to take small sips of Electral. On the evening of the fourth day, I sat up and asked Amma if she knew about Nazo. She looked bewildered.

'Didn't Qaiser Mamoo tell you she's coming to Baansa?'

Her face told me that she didn't know, that it was inconceivable to her that her niece should be in town and not stay with us. She held me responsible, of course, but because of my illness, she bit her tongue.

'It's been only Eid–Bakrid messages from Qaiser the last few years. What's Nazo doing here?'

'I wish I knew.'

For one wild moment, I thought of calling Zubi. But no, that's not the whole truth. I thought I'd *tell* Zubi. Draw her into my personal hell, join her anger to mine. Thankfully, better sense prevailed. If I knew Asghar at all, if anything was afoot, his wife would be the first to know. He wasn't like me, after all.

Perhaps Zubi was right. I did have a bit of an honesty problem. Lying in my childhood bedroom with the same green-black striped curtains darkening the windows that had been there since I was in high school, tears trickling down the sides of my temples, I considered the number of times I could have—should have!—been honest with Nazo. I could have told her about Avantika, about Sejal. Why had I not? After Asghar, Nazo had been my friend, my confidant. She would have forgiven me. We could just have been cousins and friends over the years and in time, she would have married someone else. But perhaps that was why I hadn't said anything. Perhaps I did not want Nazo to stop loving me the way she did, and I didn't even have the honesty to admit it to myself.

Thinking of Zubi, I realized that I hadn't been on Instagram for several days. I checked out Zubi's page and was taken aback to see that, along with cat videos and nankhatai in ribboned baskets, she was now posting pictures of herself. At first, it was an old photo from her wedding album, then newer photos emerged. There's Zubi dressed as a bride once again, coyly peeking through a sheer veil. A day later, pictures of her dressed up like a man, the same bridal veil wrapped about her head like a turban, and a thin moustache painted on with kohl, a saucy twinkle in her eye. It was hashtagged #KajraMohabbatWala.

The heat stroke had slowed my brain and yet, it took no more than ten seconds for me to put it all together. In desperation, Asghar had confided his play's casting problem to his wife. She may be mad at him but Zubi would have been madder yet at families who wouldn't allow a girl to act the lover on stage. She would have said something like, *These people are too much!* Followed by, *Surely, there must be at least two or three liberal families in Baansa?* And at last, *If you mount a play with no women on stage, what sort of message does it send out? In this day and age?*

Asghar would have said something like: *It sends out a truthful message. There really is no one willing.* And then Zubi would have accused him of exaggeration, to which he would have responded: *Is it an exaggeration? Would you agree? If I can't persuade my own wife…*

Thus, Zubi would have allowed herself to be persuaded. And suddenly, Nazo's presence in Baansa made sense. Nazo had a decent singing voice and Qaiser Mamoo had encouraged her to the extent of composing and singing soz and nauhas during Muharram. However, she also had some formal training in light Hindustani classical. There was no reason she couldn't compose music for a play or lead the chorus. Besides, she was undeniably pretty.

Some instinct made me check out Zubi's list of friends and followers, and sure enough, Nazo was on there. She posted very rarely, just a few snatches of song and abstract pictures of the Mumbai skyline, but Zubi had hearted every single post over the last few months.

Those years when I lived in Qaiser Mamoo's flat, I had told Asghar and Zubi about the broad hints being dropped, and the way Nazo waited up for me, the way she sat watching me while I ate. Expecting that I would eventually marry her, Zubi had struck up something of a phone friendship with Nazo. It had fizzled out once I married Sejal instead, but clearly, Zubi had not been unfriended the way I had been. Now that I was no longer a part of either of their lives, the two women were free to renew the friendship on their own terms. Perhaps they had exchanged notes on the extent of my selfishness, my capacity for destruction and deception. And perhaps Zubi had invited Nazo to come visit Baansa and offered that she stay with them rather than with my parents.

I thought about Nazo now as I had not done before. She was an only child and had been helping around the house since her early teens. Sadaf Mumaani was never a great workhorse but once osteoarthritis hobbled her, the only chore she could manage was some light cooking. Even that, she did only in brief spurts. From loading, drying, and folding laundry to washing dishes thrice a day, dusting the house, buying groceries, filling water bottles—Nazo did everything. By the time she started college, cooking was added to her list of chores. She never got to do the things other college kids did. Boyfriends would anyway have been forbidden, but she didn't even have the leisure time to go out to the movies or to the beach with her classmates.

We were both twenty-one when I showed up in Mumbai and, for the next five years, Nazo had to serve a permanent house guest in addition to the rest of her household chores. She worked cheerfully though, and listened to me intently as I told my little anecdotes, her eyes widening in shock or narrowing in mock censure. She laughed a full-throated laugh and blushed a deep pink, and I loved to watch her, especially the way she responded to my slightest gesture. She was my first audience and, apart from Asghar, my sole advocate.

The Comeback

Nazo must have expected to be transformed into a full-time wife and mother, even as her mother's health deteriorated year upon year. Even after I had moved out of her parent's home, she still waited for me. But then, I moved in with Sejal, without so much as a quiet chat to let Nazo know that my plans had changed.

Seven years Nazo had wasted on me. Then, a few months after I got married, her mother died. I felt grateful that a stage-lighting gig had taken me to Berlin at the time so I didn't have to face the family at Sadaf Mumaani's burial. Upon my return, I attended the chaliswan along with my parents, but I stuck to the men's side of the gathering and didn't try to talk to Nazo afterwards. For another year or so, Nazo and her father must have propped each other up in their grief, trying to rearrange their lives around the absence of the one thing that had given them purpose—trying to spare Mumaani. Then, suddenly, it must have been too late. The arranged marriage market is harsh for women approaching thirty, and Nazo had neither higher education nor a well-paying job to bolster her chances.

I would still text Qaiser Mamoo on festival days and he still sent back perfunctory messages with blessings for my health. Neither his expectation nor my rejection of his daughter had ever been put into words, but we both knew it for the betrayal it was. I never visited him for I could hardly look into the eyes of the man who had begun to call me 'son' as if it meant something, and who now undoubtedly thought of me as a selfish, cruel bastard. Our texts were an empty gesture that allowed us a façade of dignity; they were not a serious attempt at keeping in touch. In this way, eight and a half years had passed and now I dared not text Nazo to ask how she was doing, or what brought her to Baansa.

Mamoo had always been fiercely protective of Nazo and her reputation. She was not allowed to go out to movies or plays with male friends. Not even with me, a cousin who lived in the same flat. How, then, had Mamoo allowed Nazo to go off to Baansa to work on a play? Had he given up all hope of fixing a marriage for her? And of all things, a play like *The Rover*? Did he no longer care who said what? Did he even know that his daughter had not yet visited to offer an obligatory salaam to her aunt and uncle?

Nazo, I decided, must have been terribly bored to come all this way to work in a ragtag production. She was still unmarried and, most likely, jobless. The play must be a welcome diversion. Or, could it be that she discovered a certain chemistry with one of the other actors? Still, Asghar's decision to cast Nazo surprised me. He could have made a few calls, invited female actors and singers from Lucknow or Delhi or Rampur. Why did it have to be this woman among all others? Surely, this was intended as another kick in my teeth. First, he had showed me my place by working with non-actors. Now, by choosing to work with someone who had good reason for hating me, he was shutting the door very firmly in my face.

And Nazo? Knowing her, she would have called on my parents if only as a matter of courtesy. If she hadn't done so, it could only be because she felt awkward about staying with Asghar's family instead. Was it because she knew that I was in town, and she didn't want to see my face? Then she, too, was shutting the door in my face. And who could blame her?

As soon as I felt strong enough to travel, I booked myself a train ticket to Mumbai. At the station, I sent a voice note to Cheeku asking about his wife's health and apologizing for not seeing him before I left town, but I'd been down with heat stroke etcetera. Then I turned my phone off and swore a silent oath that I would no longer hound Cheeku for updates about what Asghar was doing.

Mumbai was bleeding me dry. I had neither film nor theatre work, nor a place to live. For a few months, I moved from one friend's flat to another's, constantly reading my hosts' eyes for cues that signalled my welcome was up. Then I'd ask someone else.

I considered asking my ex-wife if I could stay with her for a longish spell but she had taken to dating apps with a kind of droll ferocity. So unsparing was she with the details of her encounters that I quailed to think of what I'd witness if I were actually living with her. Sejal had always been a forthright woman but what was a refreshing frankness in one's twenties could appear indelicate, or worse, a no-filter vulgarity at forty. Besides, I was certain that her newfound lack of boundaries was not good for either of us. So, instead of crashing on her sofa, I met her over cheap drinks at our old dive, and confessed that I was a sad mess and begged for help.

'Your usual mess, or is this a new kind of mess?'

'The usual. But also new. I need work. Any work. Can you me get a TV show?'

Sejal arched a brow and I noticed that her brows had gotten considerably thicker since we last met. It was the latest fashion. All the girls were pencilling in lavish brows if they couldn't grow their own. I also noticed that she was wearing a lot more make-up these days.

'You and TV? But yours is a unique, internationally celebrated talent! Fresh from London, Paris, where else?'

'Pretoria. Never mind all that. Please, just get me something steady. All I want is a salary. Monthly cheques.'

'It's a bit late for middle-class ambitions, no? You're an artist, John!'

Back in the day, we had argued about the kind of work I wanted to do. I was far from picky but I had refused to do television on the grounds that it would ruin my chances of breaking into films. TV, I had said, was for those who had given up on films. Now I found myself wanting to say something about mistakes, regrets, the looming shadow of age, and infirmity. Instead, I sat in a dogged silence, staring at my hands until Sejal clicked her tongue.

'What's wrong with you? You know the hustle! Something will turn up.'

It usually does, if you grit your teeth and hang around long enough. I had been doing the feelers-out dance, texting—*I'm back, what's up?*—everyone on my phone list. I had met Biju and Sam and half a dozen other directors. I was hanging out at theatres, shaking hands enthusiastically with everyone backstage. However, a little success in the arts is like having nice shoes that pinch. Now that I'd done a couple of films and one international stage production, nobody was offering me stage-lighting gigs. The audiobooks work had dried up too. I'd been away too long and now they had other actors who did the same job for very little money.

'Not being an artist never killed anyone,' I told Sejal. 'I've hustled enough. All I want now is my own apartment and a bit of gin at the end of the day.'

Sejal pursed her lips and wagged a finger at me. But after a few cash-dry months and constant shuttling between friends' spare rooms and couches, I received a couple of calls about TV shows. Would I be willing to audition? Within a week, I had landed a crime show where I'd play a robber-murderer who beats his victims to death with a hammer. With the advance on my contract, and a loan from my parents, I managed the downpayment on an apartment of my own and all my friends were relieved.

The next update I had from Cheeku was in October. It was a picture of a newborn baby. I called back at once with congratulations, and asked no questions about anybody except Mina and the as-yet-unnamed baby. Of his own accord, he volunteered the information that Asghar had cleared his second-year exams, and that *Baanke* would be opening in a couple of weeks.

It was a clever title, hinting at jaunty heroes and flirtation. Besides, *Baanke* switched the register of *The Rover* from singular to plural, which was wholly apt. Cheeku's excitement was palpable. He'd start to tell me something, then go off on a tangent about his baby, and then he'd start to ring off but he'd remember something else that was too delicious not to tell. Costumes. Sword-play. Songs. He was in seventh heaven.

'You'll come, won't you?'

'I'll try.'

'You've got to! Bro, come on! I've seen you acting all my life. This is the only chance I'll ever have to be on stage. Why won't you come?'

I couldn't say, 'Because I'm not in the show,' and I didn't want to admit that once I'd paid the EMI on the flat and bought the month's supply of groceries, I was so broke, I couldn't really afford the flight tickets. I mumbled something about checking the crime show's shooting schedule, and he was content to hear that I'd try my best.

Cheeku added cheerfully, 'Don't worry. If you can't make it to Baansa this month, you'll be able to catch us in Delhi, in November.'

It was a little detail he had forgotten to mention in his initial excitement. Act II had been invited to Lights. Asghar hadn't even been trying to show his work in Delhi, but trusty old Professor Jha had invited himself to a rehearsal, then he raved long and hard to anyone who would listen about the delicious blend of Eastern and Western dramatic traditions that was being forged in a mofussil town, and what a pity there wasn't more support from the state, and how much of the metaphorical and literal space was being hogged by those whose only claim to artistic merit was their proximity to the literal and metaphoric seats of power. Eventually, Grassroots K. P. was alerted.

K. P. was still annoyed at Asghar for turning down

his offer of a visiting fellowship at the Academy, but he was also on the board of advisors for the Lights Festival of Drama. He made some calls to sponsors and rustled up a travel budget so that *Baanke* could travel to enter the competition. Asghar thanked him nicely, but first, he insisted, K. P. should come to Baansa to watch a full dress rehearsal. Only then would Act II accept any money.

'I want you to experience the play the way it is meant to be experienced, at the actual grassroots. You will be our guest and it will be an honour,' he said.

Intrigued, K. P. accepted and drove up from Delhi along with a couple of his colleagues at the Academy. In Baansa, they were welcomed with crisp samosas and jalebis, and then they were made to wait until sundown.

The chosen venue for *Baanke* was not the Apsara cinema, but a wedding hall that occasionally hosted ghazal nights. Asghar's adaptation of the masquerade meant that the audience would be thrown smack into the drama of a typical north Indian wedding that sprawls over three days, starting with the mehndi night and ending with the reception. He didn't even have to build a set or buy props. He used the same stage where brides and grooms usually sat on faux-velvet chairs, waiting to accept gifts and be photographed against a flowery backdrop. Silk fabric screens were dropped to suggest separate homes and rooms. A musical wedding band was handy. Veils and flowery sehras served the same purpose that masks had done in the original text. It was a proper romantic caper, full of colour and chaos and a singing-dancing courtesan. Before he had even finished watching the second act, Grassroots K. P. had offered to double the budget.

'You must do it exactly like this in Delhi!' he kept saying. 'Exactly like this! Do not compromise on anything.'

Three days later, *Baanke* opened to a full house in Baansa, with tickets going at five hundred rupees each, inclusive of snacks. The audience had been encouraged to dress up as if they were guests at a wedding. Samosas and sweets, frothy cups of coffee were served during the ten-minute interval. The crowd never stopped laughing and, on popular demand, an extra show was scheduled mid-week. Many of the audience members reported that they'd never had so much fun at an actual wedding.

When *Baanke* travelled to Delhi, there really was no compromise. Asghar refused to perform indoors on the stage. Instead, he recreated the same atmosphere on the lawns surrounding Priyadarshini. When the competition results were announced, he scooped up prizes for both, best play *and* best director. Now Act II could hold the stage in Delhi for a full thirty days. Tickets were priced at one thousand each, but audiences couldn't get enough of it. The company was set to make profits over and above the costs of housing and feeding a large number of actors and crew members for a whole month.

Now, there was no excuse for me not to go watch the play. I was still trying to come up with one but ultimately, my ex's romantic adventures left me no choice. Sejal had been texting—sexting, by her own admission—a widower who owned a plastic factory in Noida. She insisted on paying for my flight ticket so I could come along and be her wingman.

'Who knows if he's an actual widower?' she said. 'He told me a sad story about a fatal car crash. Sounds too filmy to be true.'

'Why would he lie?' I asked.

'*Duh!* To gain my sympathy.'

'Then don't give him any sympathy.'

'But now he already has my sympathy. And he's good-looking. Fit, corporate type. Assuming those are actual photos. Maybe they're not? It's the internet, after all.'

'Then stop meeting people off the internet!'

'He's worth checking out,' she insisted. 'Besides, it's just one weekend.'

'Sejal, I c—'

'Just in case he turns out to be horrible, like an axe-murderer or something. I need some support.'

'You could ask a girlfriend. Why does it have to be me?' I protested.

'Because you can go off to your brother's place in Noida. I'll be checking into a hotel nearby. In case things go well, I'll need some privacy. But if things go badly, I'll need a man to come quickly and fight him off. Besides, none of my girlfriends are interested in travelling to Noida.'

I rolled my eyes and was about to say that I didn't think I had the requisite qualifications for fighting an axe-murderer, but then, Sejal played the family card.

'Also, *I* would like to meet Aun. I've known him since he was a kid. I did invest some love in your family, you know? We got along, me and Aun, and I haven't even met his babies.'

So we travelled to Delhi together, my ex-wife and I. She slept on the plane, then argued with me all the way during the cab ride to Noida, about nothing in particular and everything in general, concluding by saying that splitting up with me was the only sane decision she'd ever taken. Then she headed out towards her sensory experience with the plastic-factory widower, and I went towards mine, at Priyadarshini theatre.

*Baanke* had truly been designed as a riotous sensory experience. The lawns were strewn with familiar motifs—a low stage with a backdrop of a giant heart woven in red roses and jasmine, curtains of marigold flowers on either side. The smell of a wood fire and fried samosas filled the air, and one could hear the sounds of silks and satins swishing past even as actors had to shout to be heard.

Male and female actors were dressed as both female and male characters, while also pretending to be dressed as the opposite gender. Yet, somehow, the actors fit into their roles quite organically, speaking in natural accents and cadences. Cheeku was obviously having the time of his life. If he forgot his lines, he made up for it by communicating in gestures, signalling to the audience that they ought to know what he's going to say, which only added to the comic effect. Shakeela ma'am had also been roped in to play a double role—she was both grandmother to the bride and the courtesan's crusty old manageress. To my surprise, even Mullan managed to pull off a convincing old-maid act, swearing to spill everyone's secrets if they didn't find her a husband among the wedding guests. Asghar himself was playing the runaway bride but the star of the evening turned out to be Zubi. Quick with her sword and hilarious in her pursuit of every skirt and saree that crossed her line of sight, she drew the most applause and wolf whistles as Captain Willmore. My eyes, of course, were fixed on Nazo. Those tinselled, gauzy fabrics that attenuated her pale, fading beauty; that strong singing voice lending her a sensuality I hadn't noticed before.

Had I been alone that evening, I would have crept away to lick my wounds at the nearest bar, but I had come to watch the show with my brother. As soon as the applause died down, he dragged me off towards the green room. When our way was barred by a security guard, Aun began to pester me to pull my weight.

'They can't refuse to admit us. We're from Baansa! This is your best friend's play!'

Aun must have known that Asghar was no longer talking to me although we'd never talked about it. I saw now that I'd have to appraise him of the situation.

### The Comeback

'Look, Aun,' I began. 'You know what happened when…?'

'That was two years ago. I'm sure it isn't a problem anymore.'

'It is.'

'Okay, then let's call Cheeku bhaiyya.'

'Aun, please. Let's not make a scene here.'

'Bhai, I've come to watch this show for the second time. I'm not leaving without meeting him. Asghar bhai will not have a problem with *me*.'

I sighed and was about to walk away but just then, Asghar stepped out, phone pressed to his ear.

How well I knew this old trick! The crowds, the congratulations at the end of a successful show, the noise backstage, the bustle of packing up—it used to bother Asghar. He wanted to cling to the high of having pulled it off, of having *made* theatre, of having thrust actors into their characters. Back in college, he would pretend that he had an important call to attend to and would go off on a walk by himself. I was tasked with discouraging others from following him or calling him repeatedly. Now here he was, using the same trick to get away from his crew.

Our eyes met for an instant and I wondered if he would walk past, refusing to even acknowledge my presence. If he did, that would confirm that we were no longer friends and that was the end of it. But perhaps because Aun was there, waving, a wide grin cracking his face, Asghar paused and lowered the phone from his ear.

I cast about in my head for words, something that didn't sound smarmy or facetious or whiny. I saw, too, that he was watching me struggle. In the meantime, he accepted a hug from Aun and slapped him vigorously on the shoulder.

'Aun! Long time! Just look at you, all grown up. A dad now, eh?'

'This was superb, Asghar bhai,' Aun gushed. 'Really, it is out of the world! I'm coming again tomorrow. I'll bring my wife too.'

'Yes, bring her. This useless fellow can babysit.'

'Who, Jaun bhai? I don't think so. We'd rather leave them with their grandparents.'

'But the grandparents might also want to come watch the play.'

'True. Maybe it will have to be Jaun bhai, after all. His idea of babysitting is to let my kids destroy the house. The older one is two and a half...'

The next minute was a haze. I heard Asghar and my brother laughing, then saying something about the festival, the weather, the costumes. I felt as if my body had turned porous, as if the words were going right through my skin, but I was unable to grasp their meaning. I snapped out of it only when Cheeku emerged from the green room and enveloped me in a bear hug.

'You came! You saw? Was it good? Arre! Look who's here! Aun? I forgot my lines, didn't I? Did you eat the samosas? Were they just as crisp as the ones in Baansa?'

As I tried to keep up with these rapid-fire questions, Asghar slipped away. Aun made as if to follow him but I grabbed his arm and gestured, no. Next thing I knew, Cheeku was dragging us into the green room to meet the rest of the troupe. I demurred.

'I can't. I'll explain later...'

'What's there to explain? They're all friends. Come, I'll introduce you.'

Aun laughed and said, 'You don't understand, Cheeku bhaiyya, he's avoiding the people we *don't* need an introduction to.'

Cheeku looked puzzled. 'Who? Shakeela ma'am? Don't worry. She's left her cane at home in Baansa.'

'I wouldn't count on that,' I said. I tried to shake his hand and say goodbye but he grabbed my arm and wouldn't let go.

'Come, eat with us. Lalit had promised to take us out for dinner one of these nights and now he's nowhere to be seen.'

'He probably saw the size of your troupe and got cold feet. It'd be like feeding a baraat.'

Cheeku laughed. 'True. But you're here now. It's your responsibility to take us out somewhere. Don't worry. We'll feed ourselves. Just come with us. The other actors also want to meet you.'

Aun winked. 'Yes, Bhai. Go on. It's an encounter long due. Sparks may fly yet.'

'Shut up, Aun.'

'There may be a conflagration. Watch out, Cheeku bhaiyya.'

Cheeku looked from me to my brother, still holding my arm in a fierce grip.

'What conflagration?'

'Just keep your eyes on him and you'll see, Cheeku bhai. I must go home to my wife and kids, but do take Jaun bhai. Just see that he doesn't get burnt too badly.'

Aun was waving goodbye and before I could extricate myself, I was stumbling into the dimly lit green room. A dozen heads turned and I heard my name whispered. My eyes were unfocussed, sweeping the length of the room. Wanting to, but also not wanting to find Nazo in that blur of unfamiliar faces. Then, there she was, sitting in front of a mirror, wiping her face with damp wads of cotton. Still pretty, if a bit rounder about the chin. Her eyes seemed larger than I remembered, or perhaps sunk deeper.

In the mirror, she saw my eyes alight on her. Did her chin tilt upwards with a touch of defiance, as if to say: *See? That's all there is to all your big talk about acting and execution of artistic vision. Anyone can do it.*

Was I imagining it? I thought I saw her lift a shoulder, arch an eyebrow, lean forward a few inches, as if she were teasing me: *Is this what you found wanting in me? Glamour?*

The next moment, someone was blocking my line of vision, shaking my hand and introducing himself. Sameer. More names followed, more hands to shake. Cheeku kept making introductions and I tuned him out until I spotted a bent figure in a chair, and another woman massaging her back. Zubi and Shakeela ma'am.

My heart thudded as I went up to Shakeela ma'am. I offered a salaam, then knelt before her. She looked at me, unsmiling, as if I was a stranger. Could she have forgotten my face? I glanced at Zubi and saw her reaching for her mother-in-law's hand, as if to steady her. No, she did recognize me.

'Punish me any way you like,' I said in an undertone. 'I have earned a hundred beatings and more.'

'It is not for me to punish anyone,' Shakeela ma'am said wearily. 'I lived as I saw fit. You must live as you see fit.'

Turning to Zubi, she said. 'I'm feeling very tired now. Can someone take me back to the hotel?'

It was half-past ten by the time the crew had changed out of their costumes and secured the props. Most restaurants stopped serving at eleven, so I decided to take them to Phoolchand for midnight kebab–paratha. It was such a large troupe, we had to split up between a mini-bus and three taxis. By the time we reconvened under the bridge, I saw that Nazo was missing.

Apparently, Nazo had volunteered to take Shakeela ma'am back to the hotel, saying that she too had a headache and would rather just drink a glass of warm milk for dinner. Zubi and Asghar had decided to join the party. However, they stood a little apart from the other actors who were clustered around me and Cheeku.

Everyone ordered and as we waited, the nip in

the air and the general bonhomie slowly unwound me. I began to tell stories about our theatre club in college. I joked about my recent stint of joblessness and crashing on the sofas of my hapless friends. Every few minutes, I glanced towards Asghar, hoping to catch his eye, but it was as if he had retreated into an invisible cocoon. He smiled at Zubi and nodded in the vague direction of nobody in particular, but he would not talk to me.

Sameer, on the other hand, attached himself to my side and kept asking questions. Was it important to go to film school? How much did Western drama companies pay? Could a small-town boy make it in Mumbai without having to spend years doing grunt work?

I shrugged. 'I wouldn't know, I did the grunt work.'

'But you must know how to manage things,' he persisted. 'You've made it.'

'Have I?'

I considered telling him that my ex-wife had paid for my flight tickets so I could come watch this show, that I couldn't really afford to treat my friends to a proper dinner, that there were nights I wanted to beat my fists on the ground or kill myself because everything just felt too hard. But I knew that if I said those things right then, it would only be because I was hoping that Asghar would hear me, and that he would relent and start to act like he cared. And if I knew this, then he probably knew it too. I was finally figuring out the twisted innards of honesty.

**The Comeback**

The crime show did reasonably well and the producer asked if I was open to trying out a different set of roles for another series with single-episode resolution. Smaller roles, these, but the apartment wouldn't pay for itself, so I ended up playing a corrupt cop, a suspicious husband, a bar owner. A short film came along, then another TV show where I played the heroine's scheming brother-in-law. Then, I got paid for an appearance at a corporate event and I realized that I was a vaguely familiar face by now. People were willing to pay to watch me celebrating a sales target milestone. I agreed to do a few more of those.

Eventually, I stopped asking questions about the length of my role, or even my screen age. I would show up on time, wear the costume they gave me, learn my lines and deliver them as instructed. And I prayed that they'd keep the cheques coming. I told myself that I had to agree to all sorts of jobs so I could pay for the apartment, and shore up against the inevitable dry spells when I'd have to dip into my savings. But the truth is, I was also avoiding being home alone. If I wasn't working, I'd start to think about all the things I had lost and could not hope to win back.

Time and again, the image of Nazo sitting before the mirror in the green room would flit across my mind. That arched brow, that teasing gaze, that unasked question in her eyes. Would she ever look at me that way again? She must be back in Mumbai now, looking after her father. Aun would have told my parents about the brief encounter in Delhi. I began to dread conversations with them too, because I was worried that they'd ask about how it felt, meeting Nazo after all these years. Worse, I began to dread looking too closely at myself.

Could it be that I had rejected Nazo because she did not belong in *my* world? The written, produced, performed world. Surely not? I am not that narrow a person, I argued with her inside my own head. I love people for who they are and not what they do. Yet, when I looked around myself, I didn't spot any friends from outside *my* world. Sometimes, the thought would come to me that perhaps I could repair that bridge if I tried, but then I would remember that when there was a chance for us to talk that night in Delhi, Nazo had stayed away on purpose. Just as well, I told myself. I couldn't bear to discover contempt in her eyes.

Meanwhile, even though I no longer asked for it, I had a steady stream of news from Baansa. There was Cheeku, of course, but also Sameer and some of the other younger actors from the company. They had asked for my phone number and it felt churlish to withhold it while sharing kebab–parathas under Phoolchand. Now I was met with a daily barrage of pictures and videos. Sometimes they texted *Wassup?* Other times, they'd let me know that they had spotted me on TV. A few of them sent a befuddling combination of emojis to convey an emotion that lay somewhere between joy, affection, mirth, and congratulatory goodwill although, if you asked me to explain how I'd worked out that a rooster, a motorbike, and a planet Earth emoji were supposed to convey such sentiments, I wouldn't know how to explain.

From these actors, I learnt that the pool of talent attached to the Act II Drama Company had grown to fourteen, and that they organized a monthly dramatized reading series at Apsara cinema. The price of entry was the same as for a movie ticket. There were about twenty-five attendees on average but, if one discounted the women of Asghar's household, the company was still an all-male affair. These readings were intended to keep the actors in a state of readiness for future productions, and to practise short skits or songs that could be sold as home entertainment to local patrons of the arts. However, some of the new actors were starting to chafe. No new productions had been announced after *Baanke* since Asghar was busy preparing for his BA final-year exams.

From Instagram, I learnt that Zubi had folded away her stage dress and, returning to Lucknow, she had ventured further into Awadhi muffins and Awadhi panna cotta with a gulkand flavour. I sent her a string of admiring emojis and posted a glowing review of her Awadhi cookies. She did not bother to respond.

The day I turned thirty-nine, I lied to everyone, saying that I was going away for the weekend. I actually spent the day holed up in my flat with the curtains drawn, listening to that audiobook I had narrated, the one that had led to so much turmoil in all our lives. Feeling sorry for myself, I ate a whole cake all by myself, washing it down with large gulps of

**The Comeback**

watered-down gin. I told myself it didn't matter how fat I got. I'd be playing the heroine's father or ugly serial killer for the rest of my life. That I'd turn forty, then forty-one, and then fifty. Sejal would marry her plastic-factory widower from Noida, who had turned out to be a legit widower and rich enough to fly down every weekend. And Nazo would tell everyone what an unreliable asshole I am, although she probably wouldn't use that word.

I had nothing to look forward to except growing older and weaker, and then one of these days, I'd die of a heart attack and lie rotting in my flat until the stench led someone to call the police. Indeed, that bleak vision may well have come to pass if it wasn't for Sameer landing up in Mumbai with a backpack and twenty thousand rupees in his pocket, and not a clue what to do next.

Sameer called me from Dadar railway station, saying he'd taken the first step towards making it as an actor in the movies. What now? It was before seven in the morning and it took me a whole minute to gather that the fool was counting on me to launch his film career. *Me!* I considered telling him to find a cheap lodge somewhere east of Andheri until he found other strugglers like himself to room with. I could have told him that the city would swallow up his twenty thousand rupees in a single gulp and then he'd have neither shelter nor ration. That it would take two or five or fifteen years, and he'd have to take up all sorts of jobs in the meantime. Cleaning, chauffeuring, car-washing. Was he really up for it?

Then, I recalled that things did not have to be quite so hard. After all, Qaiser Mamoo did open up his home to me, fed me, gave me love. Sameer was no blood relative, not even a friend, but he was a village-brother. Where we come from, a village-brother is what people are banking on when they migrate to big cities where they don't know a soul. So, I gave Sameer my address and told him to pick up some milk on his way if he liked his tea milky.

Unlike me, Sameer did have one advantage. He wasn't fresh out of college. He didn't have to wait to grow out of a scraggy teenage student appearance before being considered for adult male roles. Another advantage was that he had worked with a professional theatre group. He knew quite a bit about lighting and backstage management and, as soon as I introduced him to my circle of theatre friends, he started to find jobs. They didn't pay enough for him to rent his own place but at least, he wasn't dependent on me for food and transport. Just a few weeks later, he started showing up at film auditions. At night, he would regale me with stories of how awful everyone else had been. On the topic of Baansa and Act II, however, he was oddly silent. No nostalgia, no joy while recounting how he had felt, playing Faustus or Antonio.

I had to ask in the end. 'You came here with everyone's blessings, yes?'

He hung his head as if he'd been caught out doing something naughty, then he grinned as if I were complicit in his roguery. I didn't smile back.

'Did you, or did you not?'

'Yes,' he said. 'More or less.'

'Look, I don't want to be held responsible for ruining your life,' I said. 'Do they at least know where you are?'

'Bhai, I'm not a child to run away from home. I asked my father for one year's time and twenty thousand rupees. He just said, come back in the harvest season. But we'll see about that.'

'And Act II?'

Sameer folded and unfolded his legs and didn't quite meet my eyes. I ventured a guess.

'Asghar didn't approve of your decision?'

'Do people in Baansa ever think of anything big?'

Sameer said bitterly. 'I had thought Asghar bhaiyya was different. He's a risk-taker. But no, he's turned out to be just like all the other small-minded people in town. When I said that I want to act in films, you know what he said to me? He said, "You don't want to *work* in films. You want to be *seen* in films." Arre! Why shouldn't I be seen? And do you know what happened after our run in Delhi? There were some international producers on the jury at the Lights festival. One of the producers saw *Baanke*. Didn't understand a single word of dialogue but voted to give him the first prize anyway. When she went back to America, she wrote to Asghar bhaiyya. She said, fantastic, wow, etcetera, now come to America and direct a new show in your trademark style. Bhai, I was turning somersaults. From Baansa direct to Hollywood! Okay, not Hollywood but at least, I would be a hero in America! Can you imagine?'

I could imagine. In his place, I'd have been somersaulting too, but I knew Asghar better than to assume that he would jump at the word 'America' and he would have been irritated by the notion that he had one particular 'trademark style'. Besides, even if he did accept the offer, it was a mistake for Sameer to have assumed that he would be playing the 'hero' in any show Asghar directed in the future. And that's exactly how it turned out. Sameer went on.

'Instead of getting excited, Asghar bhaiyya sat back like a lord and began to lay down conditions. The first condition was that the play must premiere in Baansa. Only then would the show travel to America, or anywhere else. He sent back an email saying, "I am not sure what you meant by my *style*. It's just that I am located here, so I make theatre that works for audiences here. Just as Western texts change stylistically when the language changes, so my text too would have to be rendered into a stylistic translation when it is performed *in* the West." Uff! I had my head in my hands. I begged and begged him not to let go of such a huge opportunity but the man is obstinate as a mule. "Act II is of Baansa, by Baansa, for Baansa," he said. That was the day I packed my bags. I mean, there's a limit to how far one can stretch these simplistic ideas about democracy. All empty platitudes in the end, aren't they?'

I smiled and Sameer threw up his hands.

'Oh, I know you agree with me even if you don't say anything against Asghar bhaiyya. The problem is, he is like a train on a metre-gauge track. He can't handle the change to a broad gauge. One can't hitch one's wagon to a star that refuses to rise.'

I could have reminded Sameer that Asghar's train had been derailed very dramatically just three years ago, and that he had not only changed tracks, he was running a whole new train. That his wife, his mother, and his kids had had to change too. That, in fact, it was I who was feeling derailed by the track I was on. But Sameer was too young, too ambitious to understand.

'You have to take your chances,' I said.

'And I will,' he said.

A few months later, Sameer landed his first acting job. It was a tiny role in a long-running play, one of those king-and-queen folk tales with some political subtext. He was replacing another actor who had broken his wrist, but he was excited nevertheless and wanted me to come. He'd been given a couple of free 'family' tickets and who else did he have in the city but me?

When I went up to the window to collect my complimentary ticket, I stopped short. Could it be…? It was. She was ahead of me in the queue and the moment I heard that voice, I knew it was her.

Nazo was dressed as if she were reliving her turn as a courtesan in *Baanke:* sweeping skirts, a glittery net dupatta, meenakari jhumkas, and a jasmine garland braided into her hair. I took a step closer and she turned around sharply, as if ready to smack whoever was breathing down her neck, then she saw my face and suddenly, she seemed to shrink.

I was simultaneously uplifted and crushed. Nazo was right there, within touching distance, but she obviously didn't expect to see me and perhaps she would not have come at all if she had known. I saw that her hands were toying with her ticket, as if she were considering tearing it up and fleeing while she could.

'Nazo.'

Speaking her name out loud cracked open the shell of a decade. It took me back to when I used to call out her name a dozen times a day. *Nazo, is there any more rice? Nazo, just listen to this song. Nazo, wait, that's too heavy; let me carry it.*

I would have reached out for a hug if she were just another friend or acquaintance, but with Nazo, I did not dare. Even while I lived with her in the same house, I had not dared. With all the thwacking force of hindsight, I now saw that the problem had been me thinking of her as somehow untouchable. She was my uncle's daughter. My own family. *My own!* It was impossible for me to touch her without serious consequences for both of us. One wrong move and both our families would be destroyed.

Nazo seemed to have come to some sort of decision. She made for the theatre's exit doors. I don't know what made me grab her arm but I did, and she was too startled to shake off my hand.

'Don't run away,' I said.

'Why should I run?'

'Just saying, don't run.'

'I'm not running. I came for the play because Sameer invited me.'

She looked huffed. Waving her ticket in my face, she changed course and went to queue up with the other audience members. I collected my ticket and came to stand beside her. We were fifteen minutes early and I offered to get her a cup of tea. She declined. So, we stood in queue, utterly silent, until it was time to go into the theatre. It turned out that we had seats next to each other and she sat rigid, as if she still wanted to bolt.

'Relax,' I whispered. 'I won't eat you up.'

'With you, one never knows what to expect,' she whispered back.

The play started and towards the middle of the first

act, Sameer appeared on stage and shouted out one of the three lines he had. The lighting was unimaginative, I noted. The lead actor was spot-lit at all times. I pointed this out to Nazo in a whisper and was scolded with a 'Shh-shh' from someone in the row behind. At half-time, I stood up and stretched.

'I need a cup of tea. You coming?'

'Why are you doing this?' she snapped.

'Doing what?'

'Talking to me about lighting and imagination and whatnot. You never talked to me about stagecraft before. Never even took me out to watch a show.'

'I wasn't allowed to take you out anywhere.'

'Oh please!'

'Well, was I?'

Nazo stood up, shoved me out of her way, and flounced out of the theatre.

I felt a rush of blood in my head, and a spark of something I recognized as anger. Strange, I thought. Strange, but also interesting. I was almost never angry at anyone, except producers who didn't pay, and my own parents. Women attracted me, guilted me, bored me, irritated me. But I couldn't recall feeling this sort of anger towards a woman ever before.

I stood there hesitating for a minute, then I

followed Nazo out. I found her in the café and sat down at her table. She glared at me and I glared back.

'Who do you think you are?' she demanded.

'I don't know. Who was I, ever? Nothing to you, I suppose, except a prospective catch.'

We stared at each other in hostile silence that stretched into a minute, then two minutes. In that silence, I unpacked my anger and understood that I had baulked at the transactional nature of Qaiser Mamoo's offer to house and feed me. That I felt some shame about being attracted to women who were older and bolder than poor little Nazo. That my shame deepened when I saw that Nazo was utterly rudderless and unable to stand up for herself. For years, we had lived in the same house but not said a single honest thing to each other. Not even something as ordinary as, I like you. Or, I miss you. Or, what's going to happen next?

'I want a cup of tea,' she said at last.

'I offered to get you some an hour ago,' I snapped.

'So?' she snapped back. 'Has your offer expired?'

Another wave of anger rose and fell, but it was followed by an odd sort of peace. It was as if I could now put down a stone that I had been carrying on my back for years. I bought us two cups of tea and two samosas.

The Comeback

'Does Sameer know… I mean, about those years?' I asked her.

She shrugged. 'I only know him from doing the play. It's not like we're close.'

I waited until she reached for the samosa and started to bite into it before I asked if she had enjoyed doing *Baanke*. She had. Her voice truly carried the show above and beyond, I said. Had she been taking singing lessons? She had. I asked if she wanted to do more work on the stage. She'd like to keep singing, she said. I asked if she fancied herself a courtesan, the way she was dressing these days. Her eyes flashed.

I knew she wanted to say something coarse but her breeding prevented her. I doubted that she could come up with any swear words barring idiot, donkey, or dog. The thought made me smile.

'Ever wonder, Nazo, what if we had met as strangers. Not as family?'

'You'd probably try to misbehave.'

'Oh? You've thought about it? What kind of misbehaviour did you anticipate?'

She tossed one end of the dupatta over her shoulder but I noticed that her ears had reddened and she was having trouble meeting my gaze. She stirred sugar into her tea.

'And what if I did misbehave?'

'I'd ignore you.'

'Why?'

'You're not exactly a Yusuf.'

She was angled away from me, looking into the middle distance over the rim of the cup. Was Nazo flirting? I leaned back in my chair and studied her. She continued to look away from me.

'I may not look like a Yusuf, but I've done alright.'

'Good for you. Go on doing alright then.'

'But you're still here, sitting with me.'

Her jaw stiffened. She turned to look me full in the face.

'Is that what you're thinking? Poor old Nazo, still unmarried?'

I felt a twinge of guilt but recovered swiftly.

'Old and unmarried suits me just fine. It would be a lot more complicated if you were married. On the other hand, if you were married, it might have been more dramatic.'

'You're shameless.'

'Pity you're not. Still Abba's good little girl, huh?'

'There are lots of men out there,' she said. 'I could do alright too, if I wanted.'

**The Comeback**

'So, why don't you? Who have you set your sights on?'

She sniffed. 'If you saw him, you'd burn up. But of course, you wouldn't admit it. You'd just look at him and say, "Looks aren't everything."'

'Are they everything? Never mind, show me a picture. Let's check out your *type*.'

'My *type* isn't you. That's all you need to know.'

Our banter lasted half an hour. I bought another round of tea and we skipped the second half of the play. At the appropriate time, we went backstage to say a few polite words to Sameer and then Nazo and I went our separate ways.

Later that night, I sent her a text. A dagger-in-heart gif, just as a sort of test. She texted back a dragon breathing fire. And that was how, after a lifetime of knowing her and a decade of not talking, hidden from our family, something began to brew.

It took days for her to agree to meet me again. Once more, it was under the pretext of watching a play. Qaiser Mamoo no longer kept Nazo on such a tight leash these days. She was free to go out with her friends and to stay out until midnight, but no later. She was also free to travel and to sing for plays and to record film songs, as long as he always knew where she was.

In those days, she was lending vocal support to a musical production in Pune. The lead actor, she teased, was quite good-looking. I asked if she wanted to sleep with him. She called me rude, then said it was none of my business anyway. I said she was being a tease but still, as her well-wisher, I ought to inform her that the actor in question was gay. She said, 'You're just jealous of his good looks.' But a few days later, she texted me a 'relief' emoji, and thanks for telling her. I texted back to say that, meanwhile, I was not gay and was available. She texted back to say that I was just having a midlife crisis and therefore reaching for forbidden fruit.

For once I was honest. 'What if I am? Don't let that stop you from reaching for your preferred fruit.'

While Sameer went about taking his chances in tinsel town, I brooded about mine. I was officially at the end of my youth and my screen hero dreams had been blown into a dusty recess. I had regained all the weight I lost during *Twelfth Night* even though I now drank gin without tonic. I would drink in my bedroom, alone, in the dark, and often went to bed with rheumy eyes. If I didn't switch tracks soon, I'd hit a wall and implode. But an actor cannot turn his life around on his own. At least, I wasn't one of those who could. I needed a director who saw me as something other than middle-aged and of middling talent. I needed Asghar. Problem was, he didn't need me.

There's got to be something, I thought. Some way out of this deadlock. I decided to take the problem to Nazo. She had spent a lot of time with Zubi and

Asghar lately, gotten to know them. Did they not talk about me at all?

'Zubi does,' she told me. 'She thinks you a coward.'

I was taken aback. Selfish, vain, disloyal. That I was prepared for, but a coward?

'And a ninny,' she went on. 'You didn't think about the loss of face for Asghar when you went on about your silly college antics. But you didn't want to lose face yourself, didn't want people to see you as an ambitious fool when, in fact, that's exactly what you are. If you had back-pedalled, announced that you lied about the exam-cheating anecdote, you would actually have shown some courage. But, Zubi says, you have no stomach for risk. You play safe. That's what she said.'

'Uff.'

Nazo simply looked at me as if she was waiting for more, then looked disappointed. As if Zubi had been right after all. Ninny. Coward.

'I thought it was too late,' I muttered. 'And it was good for Asghar in the end. Right?'

'That's not because of who you are. It's because of who he is.'

It wasn't what I needed to hear, or was it? For once, Nazo took no pains to spare me and now that she had said it, a dozen instances of my cowardice came flooding back. The way I'd stopped talking to Nazo after moving in with Sejal. How I never visited Sadaf Mumaani even though I knew she was dying, because I was afraid of the disappointment I'd see in her eyes. That time when I got a bit part and the producer neither paid me nor put my name in the credits. I was so afraid of upsetting him, I didn't even complain. And the time my alma mater offered me a part-time job teaching and I turned it down because I was afraid people would say, only those who can't do, teach.

It was a pretty damning list and it was hard, facing up to it. But on the other hand, it was also the first time in my life that I was sitting back, mulling my own feelings without having to lie about what I really wanted. Now I knew that I wanted to become the best possible actor I could be. And I wanted Asghar back in my life. Perhaps I wanted Nazo too, though I wasn't yet sure what I wanted her for.

I might be selfish, an ambitious fool, and a liar, even a coward, but I do have one good quality: a strong sense of self-preservation. I have never been brave in the sense of wanting to take on villains and make the world a better place. I thought of myself as a risk-taker, but perhaps Zubi and Nazo were right. So far, I had been shying away from risk, playing it safe. Henceforth, I decided, all the ham parts I played on TV, the corporate events, and advertising work—all of it must serve my own goals. One way or another, I would find a way to work with Asghar again. And so, I did what I had always done. I began to prepare the stage.

First, I pulled up a list of jury members that were at Lights the previous year. There were three international names and only one of them was American, a producer called Santi. I looked her up. Mixed-race, American-Indian via Kenya, works off-Broadway.

I updated my Instagram with more pictures from my theatre work than from television. I changed my profile picture to show off my Malvolio look from the year before. Next, I messaged Santi, introducing myself and saying what a pity it was that we had missed each other at the Lights Festival of Drama in Delhi; I'd have loved to meet her in person.

Santi wrote back with something vague about how brief the trip had been, and how busy, but also, how fabulous. I wrote back saying that I had *loved* working with a multicultural team and would really, really like to do something like it again. Pity, there were so few opportunities to put together a truly international team. Of course, I stressed, it was important to make art that's not just multicultural but also postcolonial. Did she know what I meant?

Santi responded within thirty seconds. 'Yes, my thoughts exactly.' And I sent a thousand blessings upon the head of my scholarly ex-girlfriend for her postcolonial, posthuman jargon.

For a few days, messages flew back and forth between me and Santi. I said, I'd love to work with the sort of director who knows how to adapt a classic. The classics speak across the ages, don't they? I asked. And Santi said, 'Yes!'

I said, ideally, it would be the sort of text that is also recognized as a Western classic. Makes it much easier to raise money and one needs money, even if it is only to play around with subversive ideas. And Santi said, 'Yes, absolutely!'

Then I racked my brains for a script that offered such possibilities. Most importantly, I had to identify a character I wanted to play. Everything else must coalesce around that.

For a whole week, I stayed home to read. I made lists of texts with promising male leads: non-heroic heroes who need not look like fresh-faced young graduates. I looked at scenes the way Asghar might, testing the dialogue to see if it could take root in Baansa's soil. By the third day, I was homing in on Captain Macheath from *The Beggar's Opera*. A thieving rake is an attractive proposition in any language. The long-buried seeds of raucous Awadhi songs were sprouting in my head. A musical! Yes, the kind of musical that may appear vaguely Bollywood-themed to the Western gaze, but it would be far dustier and lustier than any Hindi movie they'd ever seen.

Santi would go along with it, I knew. After all, it wasn't the drama of *The Rover* that had captivated her. It was the rambunctiousness, the colour and song, the sheer tomfoolery of *Baanke*. She wanted another production in that style, and she wanted credit for it. All that remained was to persuade her that premiering a new international production in Baansa would not just be acceptable, it would be a brilliant gambit. A cultural and global first. But for that to happen, she'd first have to be wooed by Baansa.

There was a photo of me and Cheeku wheeling about in the bamboo forests near home from my last trip back. I uploaded it to Insta with the hashtags #thickasthieves and #BaansaBoys. Santi noticed and responded with a grinning emoji and a yellow heart.

## The Comeback

The next week, I dressed up as a thug from nineteenth-century Awadh and took a selfie. I hashtagged this one #thuglife #forreal #history #thuggie.

Santi hearted the post almost as soon as it appeared. The same night, she sent me a private message, asking if I had heard of an emerging theatre director from Baansa, a guy named Asghar Abbas?

I wrote back, 'College bestie. He's the guy who infected me with the theatre bug. Love him!'

She wrote back, 'Really? What a coincidence!'

Then Santi asked for my phone number and we Facetimed. She told me about her grand plan for delivering a truly authentic Indian experience on the global stage. Shake things up, you know?

I made enthusiastic sounds. Over the next few days, Santi asked dozens of questions about Asghar's student productions, his attitude towards the audience and whether it was snobbish, what I thought about non-proscenium performance spaces, and how to handle bad acoustics. Then she volunteered the opinion that, after all, the original Globe Theatre did not have great acoustics. All the great lines of dialogue written by Shakespeare were shouted out by ill-prepared actors. I told her about the jatra in Assam and the nautanki tradition in Uttar Pradesh and the forging of a distinct aesthetic identity. Ultimately, Santi said, her true ambition was to democratize and decolonize the stage.

I agreed with her, saying that was my ambition too—a level stage. Then I added a little twist that would make her squirm a bit.

'It's a classist expectation, isn't it? Racist even, that the best and most innovative artistic endeavour should be made available to elites in a convenient setting of their own choosing? They enjoy the fruits of our labour, or they reject it, or they go ho-hum or whatever! But the *source*, where it all begins, the small towns that birth great artists, they keep thirsting for high-quality productions. And all the surrounding economic benefits too, you know? The lemonade stands, the snacks, the tailors, and carpenters. All of that gets concentrated in cities where there's already a glut! It's a travesty if you ask me.'

Santi hmmed and said, I was right for sure. Then, there was a bit of a lull in our conversation. I waited three days before calling her again.

'Listen,' I said. 'If you ever wanted to do something big, and I must confess that my experience of the global stage is limited, but I do have an idea. A popular text that would be easily recognizable to Western sponsors. Adaptable characters, universal drama, postcolonial twist. Shakespeare is always amenable to this sort of thing but he's been adapted so much, sponsors might be like, meh... But I've been thinking of *The Beggar's Opera*. It's been done just enough to be familiar, but not so much that everyone goes meh. What do you think?'

Santi said, it's a thought. Then she went silent for days afterward. She was missing from Instagram too and I wondered if the whole thing had all gone phiss. A week passed, then two weeks. I trudged to my television shoots and sleepwalked through the wily brother-in-law parts.

All these days, I had no news of Asghar or Act II. Cheeku sent dozens of photos of his baby son, Omi. It was summer again and Asghar must surely be done with his exams. What was he planning next? It was impossible to tell. I was tempted to ask Nazo if she had any news, but every time I mentioned Asghar, I saw pity on her face and so, I didn't ask.

Zubi's Insta was filled with celebratory cakes because Afsana had cleared high school at the top of her class. With great trepidation, I sent a few hearts with a congratulatory message. It took three days for her to reply: 'Message from Afsana: Thank you, uncle.' I wanted to send a gift to mark her success as a good uncle should, but then I thought I had better not push my luck. That message was neither a chink in the armour nor a melting of ice; it was just Zubi's way of showing her daughters how to be polite yet distant.

After three weeks had passed, I messaged Santi again. Just to say hello, and have you been watching the new Austen show on BBC? An actor had to be careful. One 'hello' too many could cost me a part, but too few 'hello's could blow me into oblivion. But Santi came back with an enthusiastic, 'Johnnnnn! Can I call you tonight?'

Then she told me that she had been very busy, shuttling between NYC and London, looking for money. She swore she'd get hold of it one way or another, because what a brilliant idea! Thanks! It was the perfect text, really. In fact, she was already talking to Asghar Abbas about a potential adaptation of *The Beggar's Opera*.

Within a week, Act II and Santi had come to a tentative understanding. Asghar had agreed to audition and rehearse in New York with an international cast, and Santi had agreed to the show premiering in Baansa, just as he wanted, before touring the USA.

'*Such* an interesting man!' Santi said to me. 'Did you know he's only just sat his BA exams? To begin studying literature in middle-age! He's really staked everything, hasn't he?'

Another few weeks passed before the BA final year exam results were declared. Asghar was now a legit graduate, free of the taint that I had attached to his name. I wanted to rush to Baansa to hug him. But it would be a fraught move. I could deal with his silence and anger but he might greet me with a cool reserve instead, or be impossibly polite. He might offer me a cup of tea, smile at me like we'd never been more than acquaintances, and then let me go. No, it was better to feel his cold rage. That way, I'd know that he still felt something for me, that it cost him something to hold himself in check.

I focussed my energies on keeping Santi interested in Baansa and its history. Once in a while, I called Cheeku to ask about Mina and baby Omi. I continued to heart all of Zubi's posts even if she never returned the gesture. And I continued to meet Nazo on the sly.

Nazo had not yet told Qaiser Mamoo that she was talking with me again. In fact, she had saved my number on her phone as 'Kajal'. A fatuous, teenage tactic and I said as much. She responded by putting out her tongue at me.

'You act like a four-year-old,' I said.

'You ought to have a four-year-old by now,' she said.

'Are you saying that you want to take the place of my non-existent offspring?'

'Are there any others vying for the position?'

Nazo turned her neck this way and that, spread out her palms dramatically, widened her eyes while talking to me. That day, she had done her eyes up in shades of silver and grey. I noticed she was wearing silver high heels too.

'Are you going out somewhere later?' I asked. 'After this?'

'No,' she said. 'Why?'

'So you…'

My tongue was thick in my mouth. Had she dressed up just for me then? Was she thinking… No. This was Nazo, who didn't go anywhere without telling her father, and her father was my mother's cousin, and everybody in the family already hated me and this was a bad idea. But on the other hand, Nazo had lied to her father so she could come out and meet me. She had dressed up for me. What did I have to lose?

Everything, said one part of my brain. Nothing, said the other. I stared at those silver heels extended, uptilted. I let my gaze travel up to the dangling silver skeins in her ears. She had come out to meet me without even the excuse of watching a play. Surely, she was only waiting for me to ask? Even if it was only to be a tease.

Nazo was looking at me through slitted eyes. All at once she sat up straighter.

'Don't tell me any lies,' she said.

'What? But I haven't said a word.'

'I can see it on your face. You're thinking something but you're not saying it. Just be honest, whatever you say.'

'I don't know if you can handle me being honest. Can you?'

A toss of her hair. A humph. She wasn't really miffed, not really. Was she just waiting for me to ask?

Her eyes were fixed on my face, expectant, and even as I struggled to find the right words, a flush rose to her cheeks. She had read in my eyes what I couldn't bring myself to say. And yet, she hadn't flounced off. So, then?

Then, in what felt like a single, smooth movement, I gestured for the bill, paid it, stepped out of the café, and hailed a cab. When the car rolled up, I gave the driver my home address and held the door open for Nazo. I looked into her eyes so she understood where we were going. If she got in the cab, we wouldn't need any words.

I watched her hesitate. She was having second and third thoughts. Bad timing, I thought. I was just starting to apologize to the driver when she stepped forward and sat in the cab.

**The Comeback**

Time passed and I didn't text Santi. I didn't text Cheeku. I didn't text any new producers or directors. All my time was now being spent trying to dodge Qaiser Mamoo.

I would pick up Nazo and drop her off at the musical rehearsals in Pune and before she went back home, she would spend a few hours in my flat. Each time, it was harder to let her go. One of those days, when there was no work lined up for either for us, I asked if she would agree to come with me on a little holiday. Somewhere in the hills, or to the beach. I wanted more than a few stolen hours between shows and shoots and traffic.

'What for?' she asked. 'You already know what it's like for us to share a home. We lived together for years, didn't we?'

'No, that was me living with your parents,' I argued. 'And you aren't the same Nazo.'

'Maybe not. The question is, are you the same Jaun?'

So it went, back and forth. In the end, I could not persuade her. She complained that I was being dishonest again. After all, I wasn't even willing to have a conversation that would give me privacy in my own home. Sameer had been living with me for close to a year and I wanted him gone. Yet, I would say nothing to him. This was proof, Nazo said, that I hadn't yet learnt to be honest about what I felt and what I wanted.

It was true that Sameer was getting on my nerves. He drank my gin, occasionally asked for my help with contacts. He often stayed over at the homes of his new friends and yet, he showed no sign of wanting to move out to those friends. He had grown accustomed to living rent-free in a very expensive city. Mine was only a one-bedroom apartment and his things were strewn all over my living room. I couldn't invite anyone else to stay as long as he was here, but I also couldn't bring myself to talk to him about rent or privacy. Nazo thought it was rather telling that I was more concerned about disappointing Sameer than about disappointing her. Did I really care about him more, or was I just taking her for granted again?

**The Comeback**

Just when I had started to feel sorry for myself, Santi got in touch. Asghar had agreed to a week of auditions in New York on the condition that he would also audition and workshop the Indian actors and musicians in Baansa. Could I help her find a casting director who had access to a pan-India network of actors?

My heart leaped, and then it twisted inside my ribs. Auditioning in Baansa would mean lining up with the amateurs. What if I did, and still didn't get picked?

I wanted advice but there was nobody to talk to. Nazo was an amateur herself, she wouldn't understand. She had gone to Baansa for a lark, not to win anything back. Sejal was preoccupied with her own dilemmas—should she wrap up her screenwriting career and move to Delhi to be near her plastic-factory widower? He pampered her no end, but they all pamper you in the beginning, don't they? Marriage was a trap, wasn't it? But she didn't want to self-sabotage either. Why was I telling her not to go, was I jealous?

Sejal went on and on until I snapped and told her that she should move to Delhi at once. She deserved a man who could look after her, and especially one who had the money to gift her the facsimile of a new career with a bow on top, just in case she got bored.

This helped. She promptly came to a decision to do the exact opposite, but it was still pretty rubbish for me. Sejal yelled at me for a good hour, saying she had always looked after herself, which was more than I could say. And why did I use words like facsimile in casual conversation?

I had recommended QuB as a casting director to Santi, and sure enough, a month later, I received a text about a proposed audition in Baansa. However, when I sought more details, they began to sound displeased.

'Who does this sort of gimmick?' QuB complained. 'Auditions in a village? And *The Beggar's Opera*? If you want my advice, don't bother. I'm doing this gig only because I can do it while I'm sitting comfortably in Mumbai. But I am not expecting anyone from the industry to actually go there to audition. Besides, you don't need to prove anything. You've already got one international drama tour under your belt. Why do you want to run off again? The TV jobs will dry up.'

Sameer was also riled by news of the audition. Why wasn't *he* told about the upcoming show? Why was he hearing about it from some casting agency? Was Act II hiding opportunities from him? Was Asghar saving the thickest cream for some new pet?

I pointed out that Sameer had been one of Asghar's

**The Comeback**

first pets—mentored, polished, readied for bigger things. But, he asked sulkily, why this charade of a nation-wide audition was necessary when Act II had an in-house pool of talent? Besides, nobody who was anybody in any major city would go to Baansa to audition. Then, he wondered aloud why *I* wanted to audition. I had seen it all, hadn't I? Surely I was too big for a side-show in Baansa?

Sameer had started to smoke indoors, despite me forbidding it. He also lurked outside my bedroom door, trying to eavesdrop while I talked on the phone. The rest of the time, he went about the house with a rotten-egg look on his face and declared more than once that he himself would never go to Baansa for an audition. First of all, if senior actors—and he really threw some weight into 'senior'—like me were in the running, what chance did he stand? Secondly, he wanted to move forward and upward. He wanted to be in the movies. What was the point of multicultural stage productions? I did that world tour and where did it get me? In fact, Sameer sneered, that tour had set me back in my career. Nobody took me very seriously in Bollywood because I kept running off to do clownish roles abroad.

The more he snarked, the freer I felt. Free not

only of Sameer, but also of Mumbai and of my old dreams that were now worn thin and ragged. The only thing that mattered to me in the moment was getting to play Captain Macheath in Asghar Abbas's adaptation of *The Beggar's Opera*.

One evening, I sat Sameer down and poured him a drink. Then I told him that I was going to talk to an estate agent about leasing out my place at the end of the month.

'Ah! So, you're already in the cast?' he smirked.

Sly implication, underhanded blow. Sniggering at the lowness of my ambition while hinting at nepotism in the audition process. I smiled warmly and threw an arm around Sameer's shoulders.

'Come with me to Baansa. Why don't you audition too? It might turn out to be a transformative experience. Besides, they're going to reimburse train fares.'

Sameer downed his drink in a gulp and made a face. I sighed and told him that I was preparing to take my chances in Baansa. However, even if I failed at the audition, I would not be returning to Mumbai. I had other plans for my life. I expected him to ask, what plans? But he didn't ask, so I didn't tell.

## The Comeback

They had picked a large, airy classroom in the higher secondary government school. I remembered it from my own schooldays. This was the room that would double up as a dorm for students during the Baansa district interschool sports competition. Act II was using it as the audition venue. The school benches had been pushed to the back of the room where actors sat and awaited their turn. I entered as quietly as possible and found a spot near the window.

Asghar was standing at the front of the room, quietly conferring with Santi. A few minutes later, when his eyes swept the room, he spotted me and a strange look passed over his face. A flush? A shadow? A shiver? Whatever it was, it lasted no longer than a second. He seemed to bob his head, as if in acknowledgement, but then I noticed that he was nodding at everyone who walked into the room. Had he been expecting me to show up? Was he aware of all my machinations via Insta, my chats with Santi, everything I had done leading up to this day?

I put my name and phone number down on a list that was being passed around the room. At first, I put down John K., but now that I was sitting in that school room in Baansa, my screen name on a list of amateur actors felt incongruent. What had Zubi said? Coward. After a second's hesitation, I crossed it out and put down my own name: Jaun Kazim. Let me return to where I had left off.

There were thirty-two names on the list. I looked around and saw that only five of the actors were girls. Judging from the backpacks they were lugging, they had travelled from Lucknow or Kanpur, perhaps even from Delhi. Santi told me that word had been sent out to theatre groups across the country but I saw nobody I recognized from Mumbai. I was the only one who had found work in films and television and still wanted to travel to Baansa for the audition. But no, that's not quite true. I have travelled *back* to Baansa, I told myself. A home town is not where you go to find work, it is where you return to find yourself.

Like the other actors, I was thirsty too. All our eyes darted towards an open window through which we could see a pot of tea cooking on a kerosene stove. Its bitter-strong smell was enough to send your knees knocking. Mullan stood over the pot, stirring in sugar by the ladleful until I began to wonder if there wasn't enough sugar in the mix that the ladle could stand upright on its own.

My phone pinged and I hastened to put it on silent mode. It was Cheeku, texting me a thumbs up emoji. I turned and found him standing at the back door, his face split into a grin so wide, at least twenty-eight of his thirty-two teeth were visible. Then Asghar was clapping his hands to get our attention and the room fell into a hush.

There were to be no scene readings, Asghar said. We were simply to introduce ourselves briefly and to demonstrate musical talent, should we have any. Only those who made it to the shortlist would be required to stay for readings.

And so all of them took their turn at the front of the room. One by one, they did their songs, their beats, their introductions. All eyes were on Asghar, searching for the tiniest spark of approval but for a change, I found myself focussed on the other actors. Name upon name, song upon song. Flutes and bongos and dhols. One girl asked if she could show some dance moves instead of music. Another man said that he'd learnt kalaripayattu and was willing to teach other actors his martial skills, should he be picked. A jowly youth in a checked shirt was poring over a book, perhaps the text of the play. That was how I must have looked nineteen years ago, with too-thin arms, jeans that never really fit, sleeves rolled up to my elbows in an attempt to look as if I was serious enough but, failing this thing, I could walk away unscathed.

During the break, Mullan paused before me with a tray loaded with cups of tea, and our eyes met. Her eyes told me that she recognized me, that she'd be weighing me in the balance, and that she wasn't exactly rooting for me. There would be rivals in New York too. Tall, strapping young men who could sing and dance and play five instruments while turning somersaults backwards. I drained my cup of tea and wished there was more, though my teeth were furry and my muscles were clamped with anxiety. Dare I go to Mullan, ask for another cup?

No. It may seem as if I were asserting a right to something that wasn't yet mine. But, my heart protested, it is mine by rights! *I* made this audition happen. The very existence of Act II, Asghar's determination to make drama in Baansa, his fierce rejection of the kind of ambition that made actors lose their conscience—it was all my doing. But now I was going to show him that I wasn't a mere climber or a creeper, a fluke or a flake. I'd show him, I was more than what he imagined.

When my name was called out, I sensed a little frisson at the back of the room followed by a hush. At least some of them knew who I was.

I moved to the front of the room to face a little committee made up of Asghar, Santi, and Cheeku. I met their eyes in turn, smiled a small smile, cleared my throat. Just then something distracted me. A tinkle, a jangle. Anklets? Bangles?

I didn't want to turn around to check whether it was real or just my mind playing tricks. I shut my eyes and took a deep breath to transport myself back to a concrete platform in the quadrangle outside our college building. Asghar, my best friend, sitting on his heels, laughing. I had failed to do a full cartwheel. Once he was done laughing, he had chided me: 'Why do you even want to do the cartwheel? Is the character a cartwheel or is he a man?'

I opened my eyes again and began to introduce myself.

'My name is Jaun Kazim. John K. is my screen name. I am turning forty later this month. I live in

Mumbai but I grew up in Baansa. I've acted in a couple of films, a few TV shows. A few stage productions too, but to be honest, I've done more lighting work than acting.'

Santi smiled encouragingly. The silence deepened. I thought I heard a rustle of organza behind me. Was I really losing my mind? A familiar voice, a whisper, the scratching of pen on paper. No, I wasn't imagining it. Nazo must be here, putting her name down on the list. Rustle-rustle. Tinkling bangles. I wondered if she was wearing her courtesan look again, and smiled to myself.

Someone cleared his throat. I looked up and found Asghar staring at me. For a moment, I had forgotten what I was there for.

Asghar cleared his throat again. 'Um, are you going to show us something? Do you have any musical ability?'

These were the first words he had addressed directly to me in three and a half years. I could feel him chafing under my gaze. He wanted me to look away, to focus on someone else. Did he want me to fail? No, that wasn't it. He wanted something else.

I shut my eyes and took myself back to the old days, to lines drawn in mud with a stick to explain how a space should be blocked. He had once told me to play both horse and rider in the same scene.

'A theatre actor can turn into anything in an instant. A horse, an elephant, a man so deformed he appears like an elephant. The smallest gesture suffices. Neighing is a horse. A hand held in front of your face as if it were a veil signals womanhood. You can control time, place, gender with a single gesture. The only thing that matters is your intention. *Who* and *what* do you intend to be?'

Suddenly I knew what to do. Macheath is incorrigible. He is both a warning and an appeal to women who want to believe in love. A love song then. I couldn't do any cartwheels with my voice. I sang as simply as I could, an old film song where a man is telling a woman to love him, to trust him even though he lacks beauty and wealth, and even though he has hurt her in the past.

I held my body still, turning only my neck, as if I were addressing a woman seated on my right. Then, for the second verse, I turned my neck left, as if I were addressing a different woman seated on my left. For the third verse, I alternated, addressing one line to the invisible woman on my right and the next line to the woman on my left.

When I finished my song, I did not look at Asghar. I found that I didn't need to. I could feel the breath caught in the throats of thirty-two aspiring actors and a moment later, a spontaneous smatter of applause told me everything I needed to hear. I had shown him. I had shown them all and now it no longer mattered if Asghar didn't pick me. I was the actor who had learnt how to *be*, and it was enough.

## The Comeback

What happened afterwards can be told in a few short lines. Asghar did audition many other actors in New York but in the end, he chose me for Macheath, and *The Beggar's Opera* turned into *Uchchakke!*

I had a real estate agent lease out my flat in Mumbai and Sameer had to move out. Meanwhile, I decided to live in Baansa while the show came together. Asghar did not embrace me like an old buddy although I was treated respectfully during rehearsals and was included in group banter during lunch and tea breaks. But I was never invited to hang out with him at home as we used to before. Shakeela ma'am, however, did make it a point to visit my parents on Eid and once we travelled to New York to rehearse with the Americans, even Zubi's wall of hostility crumbled.

In New York, hostility towards me would have cost

more than Zubi could afford. She needed a chaperone and a babysitter for the girls and, for all my selfishness and cowardice, she knew I could be trusted with Asghar's children. I had often been deputed to take them around Baansa and Lucknow when they were knee-high. And so, I found myself spending most of my free time seeking out entertainment appropriate for girls under fifteen, while Zubi went off sightseeing or shopping with Nazo.

Ah yes, Nazo too had a part in the show thanks to her singing and her knowledge of folk compositions. She didn't get picked for any of the major roles but she did get a whole song to herself. Besides, she was doing shadow vocals in the Awadhi dialect for some of the Indian-American actresses. Asghar had even written a new scene where she got to pout and posture aggressively before chasing me around the stage with a knife, which she did with an unwarranted degree of enthusiasm.

By now, Qaiser Mamoo and my parents had discovered that Nazo and I were working together. They didn't ask how this came to be. Abba merely raised his brows and Amma went very quiet. Qaiser Mamoo simply asked Nazo if she would be alright. When she said yes, he asked no more questions. We

**The Comeback**

could not be alone together for even fifteen minutes as long as we were in Baansa, but there were two glorious weeks of rehearsal in New York. If word travelled back home about how much time we were spending together, the family had better sense than to grill us about it.

We flew back to India with the American actors just after New Year, and the play opened in Baansa at a brand new amphitheatre on the grounds of the Aalha Udal Mahavidyalaya. Needless to say, it was a thumping success. We did a whole week's run and were fully sold out, including weekdays. Then we flew back to perform in New York and more shows followed in Toronto, Chicago, and Austin; and finally, we got invited to perform in London. We returned home in the crazy heat of May and what did we find?

Qaiser Mamoo was visiting my parents after a whole decade. When he embraced me, I wept real tears. By the end of the week, Nazo and I were married at home in a simple ceremony. And when Asghar showed up at the reception dinner, at last he hugged me and smiled into my eyes.

I suppose I ought to say that all's well that ends well. Best that this story is wound up now because if you go on telling any story for too long, it always ends in tears. My only post-script is that Zubi's Awadhi cookies are currently being marketed as a brand called Zenobia. They come in twelve flavours, packaged in round tins, the tops of which are imprinted with the photo of a grinning Shakeela ma'am holding a cane.

The Comeback

# Acknowledgements

This little novel comes from an abiding love of theatre, and also from having been part of a community of producers, directors, actors, and writers in Mumbai. But passionate and talented theatre-makers are not just based in metropolises. They are also in Ajmer and Azamgarh, and they are in Durham as much as they are in London. From them, I learnt what little I know of the stage, and of solidarity in the arts.

I owe a debt of gratitude to Musharraf Farooqi for being, once again, my first reader and literary sounding board. And I must thank Saif Mahmood for reading (and affirming for me the readability of this book), and also helping brainstorm over alternative titles, and for inspiring the 'facsimile'.

I also thank my agent Lisette Verhagen (PFD), and my editor Pujitha Krishnan, David Davidar, and the rest of the brilliant team at Aleph for their continued support.